RIGGED FOR MURDER

RIGGED FOR MURDER

The Windjammer Mystery Series

JENIFER LECLAIR

DURBAN HOUSE

DALLAS

Printed in the United States of America.

For information address:
Durban House Publishing Company, Inc.
7502 Greenville Avenue, Suite 500, Dallas, Texas 75231

Library of Congress Cataloging-in-Publication Data
LeClair, Jenifer, 1951 -

Rigged for Murder / Jenifer LeClair

Library of Congress Control Number: 2005910149

p. cm.

ISBN 978-1-930754-88-1
First Edition

10 9 8 7 6 5 4 3 2 1

Visit our Web site at
http://www.durbanhouse.com

For my mother, Lynn Thibodeau, who gave me the writing gene, provided a great education, and taught me that anything is possible if you just wade in and get started.

ACKNOWLEDGMENTS

Like all writers of first books, I've depended on the support and encouragement of those closest to me. I extend my heartfelt gratitude to all who are named here. To my mother for her fine editing insights in the early stages, and for her loving support throughout. To my dear friend, Jeanette, who, throughout the writing of *Rigged*, patiently listened to me babble on about obscure plot and character details. Thank you also for your readings of *Rigged* and, most of all, for your unflagging friendship. To my son, Brian, for his quiet support and undemanding nature; for lots of vacuuming and running of errands, and for his willingness to go with lots of alternative dinners. To Craig for his love and belief in me, and for reading the manuscript and really liking it. To my daughter, Margot —you have a fine eye for nuance, and you are sunshine in my life. To Al for always being on the lookout for helpful reference materials—the books you've given me have been greatly helpful. To my brother, Joe, for reading the manuscript and encouraging me to press on with the search for a publisher. To my brother, Jim, USCG, for his input on Coast Guard procedures and marine radios. To Lonnie for all his support over the years; your help has given me the time to write. Finally, to everyone at Durban House. Karen Lewis for seeing the potential in *Rigged*. John Lewis for his time and support, and for bringing me some good laughs in the grim final stages of completion. Bob Middlemiss for his fine editing, and for his friendship. Jennifer Adkins for her amazing eye for detail. And Eric Lindsey for his wonderful cover design. THANK YOU ALL.

Searching my heart for its true sorrow,
This is the thing I find to be:
That I am weary of words and people,
Sick of the city, wanting the sea...

—"Exiled"
Edna St. Vincent Millay

RIGGED FOR MURDER

1

A DIRTY SKY boiled overhead as the *Maine Wind* beat a course
through heavy seas toward Granite Island. Blasts of wind heeled
the ship over, and banshees wailed up and down her rigging. Her
old timbers groaned as if she were in labor but she plowed on
under deeply reefed sails. Feet planted wide on the sloping deck,
Captain DuLac gripped the wheel holding the schooner on a starboard tack. His eyes stung from the horizontal rain and the salt
spray blowing off the tops of the waves. The liquid air had worked
its way under his hood and ran cold down the back of his neck.
He'd sailed in lots of foul weather, but this was a bad sea. A bad
sea.

Fragments of the past four days flashed throu
he steered for the island. The cruise had starte
On Saturday they'd sailed out of Car
tively blue sky, the first windjammer
Bay. The passengers had donned warm
stretched out topside to enjoy ideal sprin

fresh breeze had driven them across a welcoming sea. In his mind's eye DuLac saw osprey and eagles wheel above the spruce-jeweled islands that studded the Gulf of Maine, and he momentarily took refuge in that scene. On each of those days the salt air had rung with a clarity that stretched to the horizon—wind, sun, ship and sea in perfect harmonic balance.

But this morning had brought a scarlet dawn as the ship lay at anchor off Rogue Island. DuLac had watched a swollen sun rise from the eastern sea, and the familiar adage had rolled through his mind as it always did at such a dawn. *Red sky at morning, sailors take warning.*

As soon as breakfast was finished, he had given the order for crew and passengers to raise sail and weigh anchor. They set sail for Great Heron Island. For two and a half hours their course had taken them due east, reaching across a gusty southerly wind. By noon the elements displayed something akin to a rapid hormonal shift. The sea heaved with a dead roll, the wind turned to the northeast and the temperature dropped.

DuLac had turned the wheel over to his first mate, Scott Hogan, and had gone below to pull charts for two alternate destinations in case the weather continued to deteriorate. Granite Island had been his first choice. The anchorage in Lobsterman's Cove on its southwestern shore had high bluffs. If she blew a nor'easter they'd be safe there.

At 2:30 they had changed course and were now beating through steel-colored seas into a wind that had muscled its way toward a force 9 gale. Increasingly large waves broke over the ship's bow, but DuLac still hoped to reach Granite Island by early evening. Except for his knuckles, white from the cold and his grip on the big wheel, little of the captain was visible beneath his foul-weather gear. But the gear hid a man handsome in anyone's book. st shy of six feet tall, he moved with a controlled ease that ied strength and staying power. His short-clipped dark hair a face with good bones—one that could have appeared hard were it not for a pair of surprisingly warm brown eyes. Aboard his ship he maintained the posture and demeanor suiting a captain, which frequently caused passengers to wonder what lay beneath. What currently lay beneath his impassive expression was a longing for the safety of the island that grew larger on the horizon as he steered the *Maine Wind* on an intersecting course.

The passengers had come on deck to escape the unsettling motion of the ship below decks, and now they huddled near the stern in their yellow raingear. Brie Beaumont stood alone at the starboard rail a few yards from the other passengers. She leaned into the wind as she balanced on the storm-washed deck. The force of the gale molded her foul-weather suit against her body. Strands of blond hair that had escaped her hood whipped about her head as she squinted into the rain.

A smile played at the corners of her mouth, which disconcerted her. She couldn't remember genuinely smiling in the past fourteen months. There had been smiles, of course, but only as a pretense to convince those around her that she was fine. But she wasn't fine. A bullet had changed all that. One bullet, two lives. One gone and one as good as. Since the night Phil died, her life had become a haze of pain and anxiety. Sadness darkened her soul, and wherever she went, a free-floating fear stalked her. She felt detached from people and things around her. Even the recent past had slipped into the same fog of forgotten days and months that had been piling up for over a year. Taking a leave from the department—boarding the plane in Minneapolis—the past few weeks in Maine. She tried to bring these into focus. But memories had become too dangerous because, in retrospect, everything connected to everything else, and before she knew it she would be face to face with her demons. Only in her nightmares did Brie unwillingly look back.

The wind and rain buffeted her, and again, the smile wanted to surface. She wondered why. Maybe the gale had touched something elemental in her. She used to love danger. It had been one of the reasons she had joined the police force. There certainly was danger *here*, but it was a good kind of danger. Desirable danger was how she thought of it. Over the years she'd learned to make a distinction.

Brie hugged herself against the cold. Maybe this fragile happiness was rooted in the fact that Maine held so many good memories. Her childhood, her grandparents, her family wiling away their vacation time doing nothing in particular—just being near the ocean. Or maybe it was because the islands and coastal towns of Maine were such a far cry from the seamy side of a big city with its drugs and homicides, rapes and robberies.

Brie closed her eyes and felt the spray on her face, the motion of the ship. The power of the elements engulfed her. She drew in a slow, deep breath, realizing she felt secure in this storm, aboard this ship with a group of total strangers. She could breathe here. Maybe anonymity was what she needed to heal—nobody studying her day after day as if she were a lab rat with cancer.

The second mate's voice pulled her back.

"It's bad, Captain. How much longer to the island?" Pete McAllister propped himself against the wind, waiting for a response.

"We'll make it in thirty minutes if conditions hold," DuLac shouted, estimating they were still four to five miles out.

Brie turned away from the rail. The arrogance she'd noted in Pete over the past few days had stripped away in the gale. She saw the anxiety on his face as she passed in front of the ship's wheel to join the others. She knew he was in his late twenties, but at the moment he was more like a boy standing next to a man. In contrast to Pete the captain was alert but calm at the wheel, becoming increasingly resolute as the storm worsened.

"Stand by to come about," DuLac ordered.

The first and second mates headed forward and worked their way down the sloping deck to the port bow. The approaching seas loomed above them, and down in the trough of the wave the cold Atlantic forced itself through the scuppers sluicing over their boots. Pete released one of the headsail sheets and moved across to the starboard bow to belay it off. Over on the port side, Scott waited to release the second line until the order came, and the ship started to move upwind.

"Ready about?" DuLac bellowed.

"Ready," came the reply.

"Helm's a-lee." Stepping to the side of the wheel, DuLac spun it clockwise five rotations, finally pulling the spokes hand over hand, fighting to turn the ship's rudder in the heavy seas. Slowly, the *Maine Wind* responded, moving to starboard, laboring up into the wind. The listing deck leveled as she came dead into the wind. Scott unlashed the headsail sheet and moved across the deck to make it fast on the starboard side.

George Dupopolis, the ship's cook, and the passengers moved in front of the wheel and over to the port side of the ship, which was already starting to lift as the *Maine Wind* settled into her new course.

DuLac turned to Pete. "Grab the chart on the table in my cabin," he ordered.

"Aye, Captain." Pete disappeared down the ladder a few feet in front of them.

The captain motioned everyone closer to the wheel. "Our heading will take us north of the cove. When we reach the lee of the island, we'll lower the yawl boat and motor the ship down there." He knew the narrow mouth of the cove would be hard to navigate beating upwind under reefed sails. As he spoke a burst of wind hit the rigging and the masts shuddered. "Don't worry, folks, she was built for these seas." He knew the *Maine Wind* had seen worse than this in her eighty-five years. Built to fish the Grand Banks, in her heyday she'd navigated seas that were the stuff of nightmares. Seas most schooners and captains could only imagine with dread.

Like any sailor, John DuLac had ultimate respect for the combined elements of wind and water, but, if necessary, he was willing to pit his sailing skills against a challenging sea. He was grateful that *these* passengers were all seasoned sailors. On a normal cruise, fear could have been running as high as the waves breaking across the bow.

DuLac turned the wheel over to Scott. Taking the chart from Pete, he stepped over to the rain-soaked cabin top. He swept his arm along the wood to remove some of the water and spread the chart out.

"How's it look?" Scott yelled.

"Nice and deep right up to the shore. We can tuck in close." DuLac slipped the chart under a piece of Plexiglas designed to keep the working chart dry in a storm. He rolled up two others and handed them to Pete. "Take these below."

"Aye, Captain."

Within twenty minutes they made their final course change. The rain grudgingly lessened as they neared Granite Island. The *Maine Wind* found her footing, and the wind dropped from a howl to a steady keening through the rigging. The passengers eased free of each other and worked themselves forward along both sides of the ship.

Brie removed her hood, letting the light rain mist her face. She caught the scent of damp earth and spruce on the carrying wind. Her ponytail had lost some of its grip, and loose strands of hair clung to her neck. Her cheekbones glowed from the cold wind. She turned back toward the open sea. A spectator at nature's violent show, she watched the wind building out there, shearing the tops off the big waves and flinging spray into the air where it mingled with the rain to form a watery curtain. Behind it, she knew that the ship, its passengers, and the island itself would remain concealed until Mother Nature saw fit to raise the curtain on a more tranquil scene.

"When a nor'easter hits the Maine coast, all you can do is find safe harbor and hunker down 'til it blows itself out."

Surprised, Brie turned and studied Scott Hogan's Irish green eyes. He might as well have been reading her thoughts. In Scott she recognized a kindred spirit. He had shared just enough of his background for her to see that here was a man who understood running away.

"Hunkering down has its appeal," she said. "But don't tell the others that—it wouldn't make me popular." She dearly loved sailing, but a part of her welcomed the idea of being hidden in this remote cove so far away from what haunted her. She secretly wished the storm would rage long and hard.

Scott pushed the rain hood off his head, revealing russet-colored hair that added warmth to his congenial face. "Mid-May can bring some crazy weather, but that'd never stop the captain from scheduling this shakedown cruise," he said.

"I guess filling it doesn't matter to him."

"Nope. He always takes a small group of experienced sailors who're okay with whatever May has in store. Some of the other windjammer captains find the whole thing a little...eccentric." He mulled over the word.

"Does he care?"

"Nope. Anyway, eccentric or not, he's the best skipper in the fleet."

Scott headed aft and, as Brie watched, the *Maine Wind* made its approach, coasting gracefully into the lee of the island. Beneath the high bluffs of Granite Island the ship was almost completely shielded from the strong winds. DuLac brought her onto a southeasterly course about fifty yards off shore, and she ghosted along under the cliffs in the calm, deep water.

"All hands prepare to lower the yawl boat," he ordered.

Brie turned from the rail and headed aft. All of her sailing had been done on either racing scows or large cruisers with inboard diesel engines, and she admired the skill it took to pilot this 90-foot schooner in and out of port using only the small yawl boat.

At the stern the passengers and crew were forming two lines.

7

Brie found her place in a lineup that had become codified over their four days of sailing together. Tim Pelletier, a young man on leave from the Coast Guard, and George, the ship's cook, fell into line ahead of her. Howard Thackeray, who was taking this cruise with his grown son Will, stepped in behind her. Over on the starboard deck Pete McAllister and Will Thackeray lined up, followed by Rob and Alyssa Lindstrom, a thirty-something couple and the only married passengers aboard.

"Lower away," DuLac ordered.

Scott and Pete released the yawl boat halyards and the nine men and women braced back against the force. As the lines were let out little by little, the yawl boat began its jerky descent from the stern of the ship. As soon as it hit the water, Scott went over the stern and climbed down the ladder. He jumped into the boat, turned the key, and the powerful diesel engine roared to life. He brought the boat around in a circle, butted it up against the stern of the *Maine Wind* and eased open the throttle. The ship began to glide through the calm waters toward Lobsterman's Cove, where they would anchor for the night.

George Dupopolis headed forward and disappeared down the companionway to the galley. The gathering place for passengers and crew, it contained the cooking and dining areas. Pushing the hood off his head, he ran a hand over his black curly hair, removing some of the moisture. His skin was swarthy, more from his lineage than the elements. On a normal day he'd have been down here hours ago, baking his ever-popular apple and blueberry pies.

Just to the right of the ladder, he opened the feeding door on the cast-iron woodstove—the heart and soul of the *Maine Wind* to his way of thinking. He shoved in several logs and before long the old stove came to life, popping and crackling on the dry wood. George carried a large cutting board, laden with vegetables and herbs, over to the end of the dining table that had been designed to fit into the bow. He rolled with the ship, his sturdy legs and low center of gravity making him perfectly suited for work below deck where motion was always amplified. The ship's foremast ran through the deck overhead and bisected the space filled by the table. A brass hurricane lamp hung from the side of the mast, and he lifted the glass to light the lamp. His hand shook a little as he applied the match to the wick.

George loved his work, but the last few days had left an unease in him. A nervous tic worked the corner of his left eye as he chopped potatoes and onions for the lobster stew he planned to serve that night. In recent years he'd nearly forgotten what bullying felt like. He chopped more aggressively, but eventually the rhythm of his work and the smell of the fresh ingredients brought him to a better place. *Best not to hold a grudge.* He hummed quietly, happy for the shelter of his galley. George had discovered long ago that he had a corner personality. Too much time above deck made him feel ungrounded. An open expanse of thought or sky could sometimes overwhelm him, and then he needed to retreat to something more tangible. Cooking had always met that need.

Up on deck, Brie watched as the big ship slid along under the pine-green bluffs of the island. She found the monotonous drone of the yawl boat engine a welcome change from the roar of wind and sea that had assaulted them the last couple of hours. Howard Thackeray and Rob Lindstrom had gone below to their cabins, but everyone else remained on deck.

Brie noticed Tim Pelletier standing at the starboard rail, amidships. He had thrown back the hood of his foul-weather jacket revealing a Yankees baseball cap. His ruddy face and neck spoke of lots of time spent outdoors. He gripped the rail with big hands as he stared out to sea. An aura of loneliness clung to him, and Brie, no newcomer to emotional pain, wondered what bygone event might have left him so alone.

He cast an occasional look toward Pete McAllister and Alyssa Lindstrom, who were carrying on a somewhat flirtatious tête-à-tête up in the bow of the ship. They were a study in contrasts, Pete with his light-blue eyes and wavy blond hair, and Alyssa with her straight dark hair and dark eyes. A long-time student of human dynamics, Brie took them in—male and female, youth and beauty, locked in the age-old dance of sexual posturing. Pete had lifted part of the heavy anchor chain off the deck and was doing bicep curls with it. Alyssa had unzipped her raincoat and fleece vest, revealing a form fitting turtleneck that accentuated her curves.

As she turned back toward the island Brie caught a glimpse of Will Thackeray. He, too, was watching their antics. He stood on the cabin top, almost concealed by the large foremast. The steely gaze he directed toward them had a knife edge. Backlit as he was, his eyes appeared black, and he studied the two of them with an intensity that made Brie's stomach clench. It wasn't the first time in the last few days that she'd picked up a bad vibe emanating from Will. From what she had seen of him so far, she guessed it might be petty jealousy. He'd obviously spent his college years refining the art of adolescence and seemed determined to carry it with him into adulthood. Still, it seemed odd. She made a mental note of his behavior, at the same time wishing she could escape her detective instincts for just a little while.

Rob Lindstrom emerged from the aft companionway. Here comes trouble, Brie thought. Rob, the self-proclaimed photo-finishing czar of Pittsfield, Massachusetts, had anything but a picture-perfect marriage. Fury darkened his eyes as he locked onto Alyssa and Pete. He stormed forward, grabbed her by the arm and ushered her back toward the companionway. Brie heard a muffled protest and retort.

"Don't treat me like a child, Rob."

"Then don't act like one," he said, following her down the ladder to their cabin.

Storm brewing *onboard*, too, Brie decided.

She turned back to the island, surveying the lay of the land as they coasted past it. Terrain, foliage, composition of the shoreline and depth of the water all registered unconsciously in a mind trained to notice detail. The rain had started down again, hard, and the shelter of the island was welcome. But the island itself seemed a lonely and remote place. She thought about the isolation of living here, and wondered what the inhabitants, especially the young ones, did to offset it.

Brie glanced around the deck, her gaze coming to rest on the captain at the wheel. He was the type of man she might once have found irresistible. Dark, athletic, an individual. In the grand scheme of things, few men made a living sailing a windjammer. DuLac looked to be in his late thirties, maybe even early forties. She liked the steadfast authority he projected, but he possessed the kind of rugged handsomeness that got some men in trouble. Over the years she'd had several bad experiences with men too physically attractive for their own good. There was something about his eyes though—an occasional gentleness that made her want to look further. His eyes inspired trust. Over the past four days they had revealed glimpses of a man made strong by adversity and graced with the humor that often comes from learning the lessons of adversity. It was a quality Brie remembered having, but one she seemed to have lost in the groping darkness of the past twelve months. Since being in Maine, though, hints of it had begun to appear again, peeking tentatively from the corners of her consciousness.

"Lobsterman's Cove coming up," Pete yelled, heading aft.

"We're gonna hit a wall of wind when we round that point. Yell down to Scott and tell him to open 'er up all the way," DuLac said.

Brie heard the roar of the yawl boat increase and felt the ship cut through the water with more authority. As they rounded the point and started into the harbor, the wind hit them full force. The schooner stalled momentarily, then slowly cut a diagonal course dead into the wind toward the eastern shore of the cove, where they would tuck in under the bluff and anchor for the night.

Brie turned her attention to the small fishing village that

clung to the hillside. It was as desolate a spot as she had ever seen. Positively Hardyesque, she thought, but forced herself to reconsider that. On a sunny day, nestled behind its blue harbor, Lobsterman's Cove would be picturesque. Today, though, it was a study in gray. Old fishing shacks and weathered docks stacked with dozens of abandoned lobster traps. And over all of it an angry sky hurling down heavy sheets of rain. In the grip of the building gale there was a desperate isolation about this place.

2

BRIE WATCHED THE EASTERN SHORE draw closer. She was looking forward to going below and warming up, maybe even taking a nap, once they'd anchored and had folded sail. Tim had stayed on deck at the captain's request to help with anchoring. Tim's presence had been valuable on this lightly populated cruise—he was strong, and he knew his way around a ship. He waited now as the *Maine Wind* glided slowly across the harbor.

"Stand by to drop anchor," DuLac called out.

Pete, George and Tim moved to their assigned posts. Pete and George took their position near the foremast, and Tim went forward to the bow of the *Maine Wind*. There the windlass stood coiled with thick chain that ran through an opening in the starboard hull and attached to the anchor.

DuLac stepped over to the stern and signaled Scott to cut the yawl boat engine.

Scott veered away, idling the engine, and the *Maine Wind* glided silently upwind.

"Scandalize the forepeak," DuLac ordered.

"Aye, Captain." Pete and George eased the peak halyard, depowering the sail. They moved to the mainsail and repeated the task, then went forward to help Tim unlash the anchor.

The *Maine Wind* floated to a dead stop directly upwind.

"Let go the anchor," DuLac ordered.

"Aye, Captain." Pete struck the windlass brake with a small sledge. The heavy anchor chain thundered through the hull as a quarter ton of iron plummeted into the water.

DuLac stepped to the aft companionway and called down. "All hands on deck to fold sail." He walked forward and delivered the order to the forward cabins.

It was a fact of windjammer cruising that the captain depended on passengers to help raise and lower the yawl boat and the heavy gaff-rigged sails. Folding sail at the end of the day was another all-hands-on-deck task. Brie welcomed all of it. She needed that kind of physical involvement right now. It took her mind off decisions she wasn't ready to make, ones that weighed heavier on her each day.

The passengers and crew hopped up on the cabin top and positioned themselves along both sides of the mainsail boom. The rain had temporarily slackened, making their job easier. Scott hoisted himself up and straddled the end of the boom, so he could guide the sail as it was folded and lashed off. Pete and Tim manned the halyard, slowly lowering the sail. George and the passengers worked the heavy canvas into large folds over the top of the boom and lashed it off with the lace lines. Then they moved forward and repeated the procedure as the foresail was lowered.

Brie hopped down and walked across the deck to the rail. Sailing had always held the power to renew her spirit, and she wondered why she'd gotten away from it the past few years. She smiled now, recalling another mad dash for safe harbor. It was her twentieth summer. Her family had sailed their 45-foot cruiser out of Thunder Bay, Ontario, bound for the Apostle Islands off the south shore of Lake Superior. The big lake got in a temper on their last day, and before they knew it, they were running in 15-foot seas. She remembered her dad at the wheel, totally fearless. It was the last summer they'd ever sailed together. That fall, at age forty-eight, her father had succumbed to a massive heart attack, and a bright light in her life had been forever extinguished.

"I felt you out there today, Dad," she whispered, and for a moment, she had a fleeting sense of him standing right next to her.

Lost in her thoughts, she didn't hear DuLac approach and jumped when he laid a hand on her shoulder.

"Sorry," he said. "You look like you're a million miles away."

Brie's fiery blue eyes studied him as she decided whether or not to reveal any part of her thoughts. "I was remembering another time—another storm," she finally said.

"I saw you out there today. Not many sailors can smile in the teeth of a nor'easter. Danger's no stranger to you, is it?"

Brie deflected the question. "From what I've heard around Camden, when you sail with John DuLac, there's little cause for concern."

He looked away, uncomfortable with her praise. "It's risky business believing everything you hear."

"Don't worry, I always check my sources, and the Camden consensus is that, when it comes to sailing, you're the man for all seasons. And then there's your criteria for this cruise that suggests maybe you're looking for people to share the edge with—folks who don't shrink from a little excitement."

John smiled, assessing her. He saw strength in her, maybe even steel, but something else, too. Uncertainty? Loneliness? He wasn't quite sure, but he recognized the eyes of a seeker. He'd been one for long enough himself.

"You're right," he said. "I get enough sunny days and gentle winds in July and August. That's enough excitement for most folks who book during those months. They're looking for a more relaxed experience. Most of them wouldn't be interested in feeling the thrill of the open sea aroused by a 40 knot wind. Spring and fall are my times, and I like to think the *Maine Wind* feels the same about it."

Brie looked out to sea. "I'd guess, from the way things are going out there, that we'll be experiencing the thrill of swinging at anchor for a few days."

John shrugged. "I'm hoping it'll blow itself out quickly, but you're probably right." He sank his hands into his raincoat pockets. "The first day you stopped down at the dock in Camden you said you'd sailed on the Great Lakes—mostly Superior."

"Living in Minnesota, it's the closest you get to the open sea."

"When she starts to blow, there's not a more dangerous piece of water anywhere."

Brie studied him with interest. "You've sailed Superior?"

"I skippered a large cruiser out of Duluth for a couple the summer I was twenty-five. They were adventurous types, so I got to see plenty 'of the big lake they call Gitche Gumme.' Two years after that, my friend Ben and I sailed a 60-foot schooner from Duluth through the Great Lakes and out the St. Lawrence Seaway. It was September—just late enough in the season to get some big wind. We had our harrowing days on that trip. Believe me, I have nothing but respect for the people who sail those lakes."

"They're a pretty savvy group," Brie said. "The wave frequency is higher on fresh water, so conditions worsen rapidly. The seas build fast. And Superior is cold—the average temperature hovers around 40 degrees. That fact alone would make a sailor cautious." She rubbed the tip of her nose. It had been mildly numb for the past hour, and she hoped it wasn't going to start running.

A sudden downdraft off the bluff shook the ship, and she turned and studied the rigging. "Being aboard the *Maine Wind* is quite an experience," she said. "It's like a piece of floating history." She remembered their second morning out, anchored near Crane

Island—the ten of them singing sea chanteys as they hauled the canvas sails up the varnished masts.

"It's not for everyone," John said. "But for those who resonate with it and don't mind roughing it a little, there's not another experience that will ever match it. I remember a passenger once asked, 'Is there life after windjamming?' I think that pretty well sums it up."

Brie chuckled. "I like that," she said. "There's a part of *me* that could get lost out here and never go back." She stared out at the riled ocean for a few moments before turning back to him. "So what do you do when you're not windjamming?" she asked.

"I run a boat repair business in the off-season. People usually pull their boats out in October, so I stay pretty busy from then until May." He smiled, and a network of small lines appeared at the corners of his intense brown eyes. "And what do you do when you're not detecting?"

DuLac was the only one to whom she'd revealed her line of work. To her relief he hadn't asked any prying questions seeming to sense she'd rather not discuss it. Now he skirted the issue with this personal query which she was equally unprepared to answer. She looked again at the restless waters. "Actually, I wouldn't know. This is my first vacation in a long time. I guess my work kind of consumes me."

John's brows knit together as he watched her. "In that case, I'm honored you chose my ship."

Brie took a step back. "Well, I think I'll go below and take a snooze before dinner. So, I'll see you then, Captain."

"It's a date." he said, holding her eyes captive for a moment.

Brie turned to go, feeling new warmth in her already wind-burned cheeks. She walked aft and descended the steep companionway ladder with the ease of one who'd had lots of practice.

During her four days on board, Brie had explored every nook and cranny of the ship, poking her head into the various cabins, with their owners' permission, and familiarizing herself with the store room, the galley, even the hold. She now owned a detailed mental diagram of the ship. The passenger cabins were divided into two groups, accessed by companionways at opposite ends of the ship. A third companionway descended to the galley, located in the bow of the ship.

The aft compartment contained five passenger cabins plus the captain's cabin, each with a built-in double berth that extended under the deck. The forward compartment contained four cabins —each with one or two double bunks—and a small storeroom that held extra line, sails, tools for making repairs, and kerosene for the lanterns. Forward and aft compartments also contained a head or marine toilet that the passengers in those areas shared. The hold, which contained stores of food and wood for the stove, sat behind the aft compartment, separated from it by a bulkhead, and was accessed through a hatch on deck. Two water tanks below deck held fresh water for drinking, cooking and showering.

The door to Brie's cabin was just a few feet from the companionway ladder on the port side of the ship. Stepping inside, she slipped off her sea boots and shed the yellow suspendered pants and hooded slicker that made up her foul-weather gear. Hours of exposure to the strong wind had chilled her to the core.

She peeled off her jeans, leaving on her silk long underwear—always her first line of defense against the cold. She laid the jeans on the end of the berth so she could hop back into them after her nap. Next she removed her fleece jacket, but left on her thermal shirt. She rolled up the jacket, stuffed it into her duffel and took out her warmest sweater. As she pulled the baby-blue turtleneck over her head, she winced, feeling the familiar twinge from the scar on her left side. Theoretically the bullet wound had healed, but there were still times when it bothered her. Reaching up, she pulled the binder out of her ponytail. Long pale hair fell around her face and neck. She unconsciously flipped it forward to cover a pair of small, firm breasts she'd always wished were larger.

Brie turned up the turtleneck on her sweater to cover her

chin and part of her ears, and reveled in the warmth and softness of the heavy wool. At 36, she needed her creature comforts far more than when she had joined the police force in Minneapolis twelve years ago. A shiver ran through her as the sweater started to retain some of her body heat.

She leaned against the berth, extended one leg back and began stretching calf muscles knotted from several hours of balancing on the *Maine Wind's* sloping deck in strong winds. Then she threw back the top part of her sleeping bag and crawled in. Scrunching down into the bag, she pulled it up over her ear. Through the small rectangular window that gave out onto the deck, flashes of lightning sporadically illuminated the tiny cabin. Fatigue washed over her. She lay there for a few minutes listening to the patter of the rain on the deck overhead. Soon, the gentle rocking of the ship at anchor lulled her to sleep.

The sound of arguing in the cabin across the passageway aroused Brie. She checked her watch and was surprised to find that only twenty minutes had elapsed. This wasn't the first time in the past three days she'd heard the Lindstroms having it out. Her assessment of them was that they were both insecure. Rob was constantly jealous, and Alyssa was an exhibitionist. How *had* they ever found each other? She wondered why they would spend money to come on a cruise like this when they could stay at home and fight for free.

"Rob, for heaven's sake, quiet down," Alyssa pleaded. "And let go of my arm; you're hurting me."

"You're going to stop this behavior, Alyssa. It's ruining our marriage."

"What is it you think I'm doing *now?*"

"Don't play coy, Alyssa. You can't go out to get the mail without looking for some guy to flirt with."

"You're exaggerating, as usual."

"Am I really? Look, Alyssa, I love you, and I've tried to make you happy..."

"Your jealousy doesn't make me happy, Rob."

"Then stop provoking it," he shouted.

"You say you've tried to make me happy, but have you ever once asked me what I want out of life?"

"You've got everything a woman could want."

Brie smiled from the warmth of her berth. If Rob was referring to himself, she begged to differ.

"You think that adolescent second mate is going to make you happy?"

"Oh, *come on* Rob. You really have an overactive imagination. You mistake friendliness for flirting."

"You want imagination? I imagine killing any bastard I ever catch you fooling around with."

"Stop it, Rob. *Now.*"

"You're the one who needs to stop, Alyssa. And you know what else? You need to be honest with yourself."

"I've never had the freedom to be honest. You want to control everything I do."

"If that's what you think, maybe we should just end this marriage."

"I don't want that, Rob." Brie was surprised to hear a note of panic in Alyssa's voice. "I just want you to listen."

"Look, Alyssa, we'll work this out when we get home." His tone had suddenly softened. "Just promise me, no more flirting on this cruise. Okay? Playing games does nothing for a relationship."

"I can think of a couple games that do," she purred. "You know, honey, a little jealousy is cute, but you take everything way too seriously."

"I take our marriage seriously."

The last remark was almost whispered and it was hard for Brie to catch the tenor of it. But she knew one thing—jealousy was anything but cute. As a homicide detective she'd seen the devastating effects of it too many times, in everything from domestic abuse to murder. Silence came from across the passageway. Brie decided that Rob had either strangled Alyssa or was making love to her. Her second guess was soon confirmed by soft moans filtering through the louvers of her cabin door. Brie rolled her eyes and pulled the sleeping bag up over her head. The image of John DuLac's face and form drifted into her mind along with another thought that startled her. It had been a long time since she'd felt anything, especially desire. She lay there for a moment with the thought, then shook her head to clear the image. Thunder rumbled in the distance. She stretched in her bag and willed herself back to sleep.

3

GEORGE DUPOPOLIS STEPPED UP the ladder and rang his brass dinner bell at exactly 8:00 P.M. The passengers, still feeling the effects of the high seas, began to straggle up on deck and head forward for dinner. At the foot of the galley companionway they shed their rain slickers, hung them on pegs next to the ladder and slid onto the benches behind the big table. Will and Howard Thackeray were first, sitting across from each other; Tim Pelletier sat next to Will, followed by Rob Lindstrom and Scott Hogan, who told Rob he'd get up and let Alyssa in when she arrived. Rob thanked him with an icy glare that said you're young and male—I don't trust you. Across the table Brie slid in next to Howard just as Pete McAllister climbed down the ladder.

"Hope you're hungry, Pete," George said.

"Hungry enough, but I'll never have the love affair you do with food, Dupopolis."

Scott bolted up, about to say something. Brie saw him hesitate for a moment, obviously deciding whether or not to start a row in front of the passengers. He and George exchanged a look.

George shrugged his shoulders as if he'd dealt with this before. Scott sat back down, but Brie noticed the hard set of his jaw as he glared at Pete. She guessed this'd be the last time George would take that kind of abuse from the smart-ass second mate who'd just joined the crew. Avoiding Scott's stare, Pete sat down behind the table and slid in next to Brie.

George had set the table with heavy stoneware bowls and coffee mugs. He reserved these bowls for his special stews because they retained the heat, allowing the passengers to savor their food. All the other dishes he kept aboard were enameled aluminum, just right for serving meals up on deck while they were under way. Carrying a tray over, he placed two carafes of coffee, crocks of butter and two pots of honey in the center of the table. "Help yourselves to the coffee," he said. "There's more brewing."

Brie poured herself a cup and passed the carafe to Howard. She leaned back, enjoying the warmth of the mug in her hands, and breathed in the coziness around her. Brass hurricane lamps lit the ship's galley, their glow reflecting off the golden oak of the table and the interior. The color alone might have warmed the weary sailors even without the help of Old Faithful, radiating heat into the room from its little alcove in the corner of the galley. George had told her that he'd given the stove its name his first season aboard the *Maine Wind*. "Old Faithful adds a bit of magic to every meal I cook," he had said.

Alyssa Lindstrom was the last passenger to arrive. Everyone else had been wearing rain slickers when they descended into the galley, but Alyssa carried an umbrella, equipment unheard of on a windjammer. She collapsed it, shaking off the water, and came down the companionway ladder backwards, wearing a pair of blue jeans that looked like they were painted on and a red sweater that carried out the same theme. The effect was instantaneous—all the male heads whipped around to take in the view.

Brie could almost see the smoke starting to rise from Rob's ears as his hands curled into fists. She had noticed that Alyssa's presence worked like a catalyst, setting off chain reactions wherever she went. Her tight clothes got men's attention; men's attention made Rob jealous; Rob's jealousy bolstered Alyssa's flagging self-esteem and encouraged her to provoke him some more. The cycle endlessly repeated itself. Over the last four days Alyssa had systematically tested her chemistry on each man aboard with varying results, but Rob's reaction was a constant. He was a study in sustained rage.

"Here you go, Alyssa," Scott said, standing up and motioning her in next to her husband. Alyssa set her umbrella down under the rain slickers, slid in next to Rob and snuggled up to his shoulder.

"Sorry I'm late, honey, I was straightening up in the cabin. Things really got thrown around during the storm." She looked across at Pete. Rob, in what seemed to Brie like an uncharacteristic gesture, put his arm around Alyssa and drew her closer to him. Despite his jealousy, or maybe because of it, Brie had noticed he wasn't demonstrative with his affection.

"The captain should be down in a few minutes," Scott said to George. "He was organizing some charts that got pulled out today when things started to get wild." Howard Thackeray spoke from his corner up in the bow. "I guess it'll be a couple of days before this thing blows itself out."

"I think we can depend on that, the way things were building out there today," Scott said, trying his coffee. "It's one of the best times of the year for sailing, but one of the worst for predictable weather."

"I knew something like this would happen when I decided to take this cruise." Will Thackeray sat sullenly in the corner, acting like a whiney 14-year-old. He wore his light brown hair in a buzz cut, which did nothing to soften his sour expression.

"Okay, Eeyore," his father chided. "Remember we're all having the same gloomy day."

Pete reached for one of the carafes and poured himself another steaming mug-full. "So, any suggestions for fun or profitable ways to pass a couple days if we're stuck here at Granite Island?" He gave Brie a wink as he passed the carafe to her.

"I know a little about this island," said Tim Pelletier. "There are some good hiking trails leading up to the bluffs on the far side."

"Oh, great! Hiking in the rain," Will sniffed.

Tim stared into his coffee cup.

"Take it easy, Will," Pete interjected. "Obviously, Tim meant that we could hike if the rain lets up."

"Don't tell me what to do, McAllister," Will snapped. "You're one person I'm not taking any orders from."

"I love walking in the rain," Alyssa spouted randomly.

Brie could see those miniature video screens behind all the men's foreheads light up with the image of Alyssa, in the rain, wearing her current outfit. Rob's eyes narrowed homicidally as he picked up the vibrations.

George set down two baskets filled with hot buttermilk biscuits he'd just pulled out of the oven. "Dig in folks; there's another pan on the way." Hands immediately shot out, and within seconds everyone was digging a knife into the butter or drizzling honey from a pot onto a warm biscuit. Ah, food, Brie thought. The great silencer.

Unfortunately, the silence was short-lived. With a mouth full of biscuit, Rob salvoed off the next disagreeable comment. "So, Ms. Beaumont, you look like one of those chicks who's always thinking. Any suggestions on what to do here?"

Brie stared at him for a second before deciding to rise to the bait. "Just one, Rob. I suggest that thinking should always precede speaking."

Scott suppressed a laugh.

"Rob doesn't like it when people think too much," Alyssa said, studying the ceiling over the table. "He's more into action."

"That's not true, Alyssa. I just think people take things too far, if you know what I mean." He looked at her sweater.

Fortunately, at that moment John DuLac came tramping down the ladder with several charts stuffed under his raincoat. "Sorry I'm late, folks. Revoltin' turn of events with this weather, eh?" He set the charts in the corner, hung up his coat and slid onto the bench next to Pete. "George, I hope you're not waiting dinner for me—everyone must be starved."

"Oh, they're not suffering, Captain. They just polished off two carafes of coffee and a dozen biscuits. You'll have to wait for the next batch." As he spoke, he carried the soup pot over to the table and set it on a wooden board. He ladled out large servings of lobster stew into the deep bowls and handed them around the table. When everyone was served, including himself, George took the big pot back to the stove. He pulled the next round of biscuits out of the oven and refilled the baskets. Then he set down two boards filled with various cheeses along with two bowls of fresh fruit. "Just to ward off scurvy," he joked, sliding onto the bench next to John.

Everyone dug in, and for the next few minutes nothing but satisfied sounds rose from the contented sailors as they consumed their stew along with slabs of cheese and warm crumbly biscuits. The stew was thick with big chunks of claw and tail meat floating in a sumptuous cream sauce.

"George, you've outdone yourself," Howard said, looking down the table so he could see the cook. "This is the best lobster stew I've ever tasted."

"Just doing my job," George mumbled, somewhat flustered by the praise.

"George, this stew is way beyond the call of duty," John said, smiling.

Pete spoke up as if he wanted to divert the focus from George. "Jeez, Captain, you were amazing out there today. Last year, on the *Yankee Pride,* I never experienced anything like that. I was trying to figure out how you stay so cool during a storm like that."

"Pete, it's not your job to analyze anything when we're in a gale. If you haven't sailed enough to have instincts, then you follow orders—nothing else," DuLac said matter-of-factly.

The captain went back to eating his stew, but Rob, not about to miss the opportunity to goad Pete, feigned little kisses in his direction. Pete's eyes darkened with anger as he glared back. Rob laughed and cuddled closer to Alyssa.

Scott decided to move things in a different direction. "So, Captain, you planning to teach a class in chart reading tonight?" he asked, nodding toward the long, paper cylinders that John had stacked in the corner.

"Those charts got wet up on deck today," DuLac said. "I'm going to hang them in the galley near the stove so they'll dry."

"That's not a bad idea, though," Pete said, his anger dissipating "Before you came in, Captain, we were talking about possible ways to pass a couple of stormy days. Maybe some of the passengers would like to hone their navigation skills."

"We could do some plotting using a chart with a compass rose and the parallel rulers," Scott said.

Alyssa eagerly joined in. "That would be great. I've always wanted to learn more about navigation."

"Wonderful!" Will muttered. "So now, instead of having the experience we paid for, we get to play at it."

"I can teach you all you need to know about that stuff, Alyssa," Rob said. "You don't have to waste the captain's time."

Alyssa colored and stared at her coffee cup.

John was mystified. Mostly his customers were happy with whatever the Maine skies and George dished up. These people were all sailors, and, frankly, he was confused by their attitude considering this afternoon's excellent adventure. He'd never dealt with such an odd group—particularly on his shakedown cruise. Will was sarcastic and antagonistic. Rob was constantly on the lookout for prospective flirters. Howard seemed mildly confused about why he was here at all, and Tim was so silent he was completely unknowable. Brie was running away from something and kept herself well concealed. And Alyssa? If there was a genuine person there, she was hard to reach behind the provocative facade. John looked around the table. He was beginning to have reservations about the rest of this cruise. And now that they were stuck here in the gale, his reservations had, for some reason, turned to apprehension.

The sound of a boat motor roused John from his thoughts.

"Ahoy, the *Maine Wind*," was barely heard over the motor and the wind.

DuLac nodded toward the ladder. "Scott, go topside and check that out."

"Aye, Captain." Scott slid out from behind the table, grabbed his slicker and climbed up the ladder. The rain was coming down hard. Pulling his hood up, he headed over to the port rail and walked aft to where a lobsterboat sat idling as it bobbed up and down in the water.

"Ahoy there," Scott shouted. "What can we do for you?"

A woman's voice carried over the noise of the engine. "Just wonderin' if your cook could use some lobsters? Hard shells—I'll sell them to ya at four bucks apiece."

With both rain and darkness falling, Scott hadn't realized the oilskinned visitor was female. Surprised, he called back, "You're working late on a wicked night. You should be home by your fire."

"Just thought I'd get to you before the competition."

"This your lobsterboat?"

"It's mine all right."

Scott marveled at the tenacity of those who eked a living from the sea, sometimes under dreadful conditions. He'd often heard Captain DuLac express his respect for the dangerous work they did and knew the captain counted many friends among the lobstermen. Coming from his privileged background, Scott couldn't imagine the hardship of their work—the long cold hours at sea in all kinds of weather with no guarantee of income. Yet he knew these fishermen wouldn't have traded their work. It was generational—in the blood.

Pete arrived on deck and joined Scott at the rail. "Ahoy there," he shouted and waved to the fisherman. Anna Stevens, busy keeping her boat a safe distance from the *Maine Wind*, waved from the wheelhouse but didn't try to communicate.

"Pete, call down and see if George wants some lobsters at four bucks each." Pete walked to the companionway and yelled down.

"Hey, George. Can you use some lobsters at four bucks apiece? There's a fisherman up here wants to know."

George polled the crowd. "Whataya say, folks? Can you stand any more lobster?"

There was a chorus of assent.

"Why else would we come to Maine?" Rob blurted out. "They've got windjammers in the Caribbean, you know."

Brie amused herself with the thought that if you reverse the letters in "Rob" you get "Bor." His demeanor shed light on Alyssa's antics. After all, Brie thought, one act of insensitivity probably begets another.

"Tell him we'll take a baker's dozen, Pete," George called back. "Come on down; I'll give you the money."

Pete descended to the galley, where George gave him money in a zipper baggie that had a couple of stones in it for weight. "Throw that down to the fisherman," George said.

In the meantime Scott had gone down to the storeroom and retrieved a creel to hold the lobsters. He headed back aft and descended to the yawl boat. Anna motored slowly to the stern of the *Maine Wind* and counted thirteen good-sized lobsters into the creel. Scott tied it to the ship, where it hung submerged in the water.

Pete arrived with the money, threw it down to Scott and quickly headed back to the shelter of the galley. Scott passed the baggie to the woman. She dropped it into her raincoat pocket, walked back to the wheel house and motored through the thick rain toward shore.

Down in the galley, the passengers slouched contentedly at the table, sipping coffee. George's stew had worked like a drug, dispelling some of the pre-dinner edginess. In Pete's absence, John had moved down next to Brie and was chatting quietly with her.

George was in the galley, mounding chocolate chip cookie dough onto baking sheets. He opened the feeding door on Old Faithful and shoved in a log to keep the oven temperature up.

Scott came back down the ladder, fresh from his lobster trading. He peeled off his rain slicker and hung it up. Scott was less flamboyant than Pete but better looking, and Brie wondered from which side of his family he'd inherited his lively green eyes and red hair.

"It's getting dark topside, Captain," Scott said. "Should Pete light the lanterns?"

Surprised, DuLac checked his watch. The time was 9:05. "I didn't realize it was so late. Take care of it, Pete."

Pete started up the ladder, paused and turned around. "Has anyone seen my marline spike?" he asked. "I used it to unjam a line this afternoon during the storm. It may have fallen out of my belt on the deck somewhere."

No one had seen it.

"I'll keep an eye out for it, Pete," Scott said. "We've got a couple of spares down in the storeroom. Why don't you grab one?"

"Will do." Pete continued up the ladder.

Scott sat back down and filled his coffee mug. He stretched out his legs and leaned his head back.

Howard spoke to him from the far end of the table. "So, Scott, are we going to be treated to a short concert tonight?"

"I'm game if everyone else is," Scott said.

"No rush, though," Howard added. He nodded his round bald head encouragingly toward Scott. "You just enjoy your coffee and warm up."

When Pete came back down, he noticed the captain had taken over his place next to Brie. "Say, Captain, I'd love to reclaim my spot," he said winking at Brie.

"Too late, Pete. You forgot to say 'quack quack seat back,' " George grinned.

"Don't be annoying, Dupopolis."

"Knock it off, Pete, and sit down. You're not getting your spot back," DuLac said.

Brie had run into lots of guys like Pete whose flirting knew no bounds. But she noticed Alyssa looked flustered, as if she expected Pete's attentions to be reserved for her alone.

"If the storm doesn't let up, we'll go onto the island tomorrow," DuLac said, letting out a yawn. "I know the people who own the Snug Harbor Bed and Breakfast. For a small fee everyone can get a nice hot shower, and Betty serves a mean cup of coffee along with some of the best blueberry and apple cobbler in Maine. This time of year their place is usually empty, and they won't mind if we make ourselves at home. They've got a great library with a fireplace and plenty of comfortable furniture.

"Do they have anything like a TV?" Will asked sullenly.

"*There's a TV room* with a pretty good video collection. There's also a pool table and lots of other games and activities. It's a nice place to hang out on a rainy afternoon."

While the captain was talking, Scott had retrieved his guitar from the crew's sleeping area behind the galley.

Brie had been impressed by his ability when he played the night before. She'd asked him about his training and received a brief history of his life. Scott had grown up in Providence, Rhode Island, the son of a wealthy doctor, and had begun studying violin at age six. By the time he was eighteen, he sat as concertmaster in one of the top youth symphonies in the country.

"I was supposed to attend Harvard that fall, and after that, medical school. My father had it all planned out."

That August Scott loaned his $30,000 violin to a friend whose family would never be able to afford an instrument to match their son's talent. He bought an acoustic guitar, some guitar books, and a used Chevy Blazer. Leaving the keys to his Beemer along with a letter to his mother, he took the highway north to Maine. "That was seven years ago, and they've been the happiest seven years of my life," he had said.

Scott pulled a stool up to the end of the table and began tuning his guitar. He reminded everyone that this was not a concert but background music, and that they should feel free to visit with one another.

Brie was mesmerized by the mellow tones of the guitar filling the cozy galley, mingling with the crackling wood in the stove and the howl of the wind outside the ship. She relaxed into the yellow glow thrown off by the hurricane lamps in the low-ceilinged space, and the smell of cookies baking in the oven wrapped itself around her like a warm blanket. This experience alone was worth the price of the ticket.

Scott began with some folk selections, moving on to classical and jazz pieces after he warmed up. As he played, some of the tension around the table dissolved, and quiet conversations started up. He was happy to see his music become the backdrop for a more amiable scene.

Brie ventured into conversation with Tim, who was sitting across from her. She hoped to draw him out a bit. He'd been virtually silent the past few days.

"You mentioned on the first day out that you're in the Coast Guard," she said. "Are you new to the service?"

"Pretty new. I just finished training in my specialty, and I'll be heading for my first assignment in two weeks."

"Why did you choose the Coast Guard?" she asked.

"They save lives." His response was immediate and intense. Then, as if to soften it, he added, "But the main reason is I've lived near the ocean all my life. I couldn't stand to be far from the water."

"What specialty did you train for?" Brie asked.

32

"Marine Science Technician."

She noticed the note of pride in his voice. He seemed to gradually warm to the conversation, once he got over his surprise at someone showing an interest in him. Brie was used to the fact that with most men, especially young ones, there were few reciprocal questions. Conversation usually felt more like interrogation. That was fine with her; the fewer questions she had to answer about herself right now, the better.

"So where's your first assignment?" she asked.

"Coast Guard Station Juneau. In Alaska."

"That's a long way from home."

A faraway look came over him, and behind it, Brie sensed an intense emotion. Sadness, pain, regret? A moment later it was gone, like the lid snapping shut on a tightly hinged box.

"I need to visit new places," he said emphatically. "It's bad to stay in one place all your life."

Brie noted the use of "need" rather than "want" and wondered what drove that need.

George had pulled two large cookie sheets out of the oven, and they had been sitting with the cookies cooling for the past few minutes. The smell of butter, sugar and chocolate filled the galley. Finally, DuLac spoke up.

"George, you shouldn't keep chocolate chip cookies from a man who's sailed through a gale. So serve 'em up now, or I won't be held accountable for my actions."

"Sorry, Captain. Let me grab my spatula—I wouldn't want to lose a hand passing them out."

George ladled out the goods, and within fifteen minutes, the cookies were gone, along with doses of brandy the captain administered to anyone who was interested.

Scott continued playing for a while, but the evening was winding down. It was almost ten o'clock on what had been a draining day for all present. Rob Lindstrom and John had actually leaned their heads back and dozed off. Brie was starting to feel as if she might have to be carried to her cabin on a stretcher. Alyssa and Pete were eyeing each other in a high-risk flirtation, considering Rob's hair-trigger temper. Tim had pulled out a pocketknife and a piece of wood and was whittling away at it, happy that it kept him from too much human interaction.

Suddenly Rob lunged across the table. "Keep your eyes off Alyssa, you sonofabitch!" An index finger jabbed threateningly at Pete.

Pete stared at him defiantly. "Hey, man, get a grip!"

"You're playing a dangerous game," Rob growled. The finger jabbed again. "Don't mess with my wife."

The captain brought the flat of his hand down on the table. "That will do, gentlemen! McAllister! Topside, now. Check out the lanterns and the anchor."

Pete almost trampled George getting past him and up the companionway.

"There will be no threats or animosity on this cruise. Is that clear?"

Rob glared at the captain but said nothing.

DuLac continued. "The rest of the passengers have a right to the atmosphere they paid for. I'll not tolerate a troublemaker on my ship." The captain's eyes held Rob in a steely gaze.

"Then you'd damn well better keep your crew in line, Captain." Rob nodded to Alyssa. "Let's go. Time to turn in." They slid out from behind the table, and Rob pawed through the rain slickers until he found his.

"Rob, could I borrow your raincoat? I'm a little cold."

"Oh, Alyssa, for Christ's sake." Rob peeled off his slicker and handed it to her. "Give me that thing," he said, grabbing the umbrella. "Here, George, make this disappear before it embarrasses me to death. Maybe you can chop it up and use it as a garnish." He stormed up the companionway ladder with Alyssa following behind.

The remaining passengers and crew surveyed one another in stunned silence. "And here, all along, I thought the guitar was a calming instrument," Scott said, dispelling some of the tension.

"We need to set the watch," DuLac said, eager to wrap things up. "You take the first watch from 2200 to 0100 hours. Pete already asked about his watch and knows he's on from 0100 to 0400, when I'll come on deck to relieve him."

"Sounds good, Captain. I'll go topside and tell Pete to hit the sack."

Scott disappeared into the crew's sleeping area, where he stowed his guitar. He pulled on the pants to his foul-weather suit, hiked the suspenders up over his shoulders and headed back out to the galley to grab his rain jacket.

"There'll be a fresh carafe of coffee down here, as usual," George said.

Brie spoke up. "Thanks for the concert, Scott; it was great." Howard seconded her enthusiastically.

"My pleasure, folks," Scott said, heading up the ladder.

"I think everyone can safely sleep in tomorrow," John said. "This rain and wind is likely to hang around for a day or two. George, you may as well plan breakfast for an hour later than usual."

"No arguments from me on that, Captain."

"I'll pass the word to Rob and Alyssa when I go down," Brie said.

"You're a brave woman, Brie," Howard said, patting her arm in a fatherly manner.

On that note, everyone slid out from behind the table, donned their rain slickers and said a hasty goodnight to the captain before climbing the companionway ladder. Up on deck, cold wind and rain assaulted them. Their hunched forms shone eerily in the yellow light cast by the hurricane lanterns that swung from the rigging. They made their way along the rain-soaked deck and descended into the belly of the ship, heading for their cabins and warm sleeping bags.

At the foot of the ladder Brie stepped over and knocked on

the cabin door directly across from hers.

Alyssa's voice came through the louvers. "Who is it?"

"It's Brie. Just wanted to let you know that breakfast will be an hour later than usual. So you can sleep in."

"Thanks, Brie; we'll see you in the morning. Sleep tight."

"Good night," said Brie.

Inside her cabin, Brie wasted no time in her nightly routine. She drew off a basin of water from the wooden cask that sat up on a small shelf in the corner of the cabin. Grabbing her soap, she washed her face. Then, leaning over the bowl with cupped hands, she shivered as the cold water splashed the soap away. She held the soft hand towel against her skin for an extra moment, warming her face, then filled her small cup with water from the cask and brushed her teeth. The cold water felt better in her mouth than it had on her face, and she swished it around a few extra times before spitting into the wash basin. The basin would sit there until morning, when she'd go up on deck and throw its contents overboard.

Brie sat down on the berth, pulled her weather radio out of the duffel and switched it on. She was hoping to hear a report on the storm, but got only crackly static. Suddenly her vision blurred. Nausea dampened the back of her neck and she felt the familiar grip of panic as she spun back to *that night*.

"All units—460 in progress, 3147 Upton Avenue North."

Brie grabbed the receiver. "Unit 14 responding." Her arm pressed hard against the door as Phil spun the car around and headed back the opposite direction.

"Code 2," the dispatcher's voice crackled, advising no lights no siren.

"Ten-four." Brie glanced over at Phil as she replaced the receiver. She knew he was eager to get home. His son was sick and his wife would be tired. "Sorry, Phil."

"Hey, when it rains, it pours."

They'd just left the scene of a homicide less than a mile away and had joked about making it home before the witching hour. It wasn't likely to happen now.

The bronze Crown Victoria made its stealth approach, drawing silently up to the curb in front of a two-story duplex. The warm breeze that ushered them up to the gaping door carried a promise of spring. Guns drawn, they paused to make eye contact before slipping into the darkness beyond.

Just inside the door a rank smell of body sweat and stale cigarettes assaulted them. They stood for a moment barely breathing, letting their eyes adjust to the dark. Phil motioned his gun toward the doorway on the opposite wall, signaling her to check it out, and turned his attention to the door on his left. Too late, she glimpsed movement. Deafening sound and searing pain struck her in the same instant. Then slow motion. Phil falling, screaming from somewhere, the floor rising toward her and darkness.

A flash of lightning filled the cabin. Brie looked around, disoriented, trembling. For a moment she thought she was back in the hospital. Her hands shook as she squatted down and dug into her duffel. She brought out her off-duty pistol—a Glock 9mm—and clip-on holster. Before the cruise, when she'd told the captain she was a police officer, she had asked his permission to bring the gun aboard. Having it with her, even on vacation, was one of the ways Brie tried to convince herself that she felt safe. In reality, she hadn't felt safe for a long time.

She checked the clip and chamber and sat down on her berth. She turned the gun over in her hands debating. Finally, she slipped it into the holster and placed it under her pillow. Still shaking, she crawled, fully clothed, into her sleeping bag and zipped it all the way up. The rain drummed steadily on the deck overhead. After a while its rhythm began to calm her. She thought back on the scene after dinner and, as she drifted toward a restless sleep, wondered how they were going to survive peacefully here until this gale blew out.

4

AT THREE-FIFTEEN IN THE MORNING Brie jolted awake, shaken by a scream deep within her. The echo of it clung to her as she sat up. Sweat sheened her body, and the cold hand of death wrapped itself around her heart, squeezing. Her fingers went unconsciously to her side, to the spot where the bullet had entered. She drew in a deep breath of the cold salt air, trying to slow her racing heart. As she listened to the rain pummeling the deck, she heard footsteps overhead.

"Pete! What's going on?" DuLac shouted.

Alyssa's frightened voice shot through the darkness. "Up here."

Brie jumped off her berth, realizing the scream was no invention of her unwelcome dreams. She clipped her gun onto her jeans and grabbed her raincoat off its peg as she headed out the door. She nearly collided with Rob as he rushed into the narrow passageway from the cabin opposite hers.

"That was Alyssa!" He bolted up the ladder with Brie right

behind him. As they hurried toward the bow, lightning strobed illuminating a grisly scene. Pete McAllister lay on the deck, arms and legs splayed, a marline spike protruding from his chest.

Alyssa Lindstrom was sobbing in the captain's arms. Hiccups of emotion racked her as she forced out her story. "I couldn't sleep...I came on deck to have a cigarette...and found him like this ...I know we're not allowed to smoke on board, Captain...I'm sorry." Her confession sounded desperate, as if taking back that cigarette might somehow reverse the course of events.

Brie squatted down next to Pete to check for a pulse, but the coldness her fingers touched immediately told her there'd be none. In the next flash of lightning she found DuLac's eyes.

"He's dead," she said, against the wind.

As Brie bent over Pete's lifeless form, lightning split the sky, glinting coldly off the marline spike lodged in his chest. A syrupy stream of blood ran from the weapon down the side of his yellow raincoat to pool unseen beneath his body. The screams that had awakened the captain, Brie and Rob soon brought Scott, George and Tim up on deck.

"Jesus Christ! What the hell happened here?" Scott's voice jumped up a range.

"Is he...dead?" George forced out the last word.

Tim looked on in stunned silence.

Will and Howard Thackeray arrived last. "What's going on?" Will demanded, pushing past everyone.

The others pressed closer to the body.

"Pete's dead."

"Pete's been murdered."

"Murdered! Who says he was murdered?" George's voice broke.

"What do you think, he committed suicide by stabbing himself in the chest? Get real, Dupopolis," Will jeered. "And there's a rope around his neck. Do you think he strangled himself and, when it wasn't working, he went for the marline spike?"

"Stuff a sock in it, Will," Brie snapped. "And everybody step back, right now."

"Why's she giving the orders?" Rob scoffed.

DuLac began moving the group back from the body. "This isn't the time or place for your antagonism, Rob," he said. "It just so happens Brie is a homicide detective on leave from the Minneapolis Police Department. We're extremely lucky to have her with us, and whatever she requests, you *will* do. Now, step back."

Another buzz of surprise ran through the group as they craned their necks to see what Brie was doing.

Although they'd been sailing together for four days, Brie had not mentioned her exact line of work to anyone but the captain, making it clear to him that she preferred not to share that fact with the rest. When asked, she had simply said that she was employed by the city of Minneapolis in what she referred to as a public relations job.

She stood up now and came over to the passengers.

"I know this is a shocking situation, but it's 3:30 in the morning and there's not much we can do until daylight. It would be best if you all went back to your cabins and tried to get some sleep. The captain and I will be up here for awhile; I need to take some pictures and make notes on the crime scene before we can cover the body."

"Crime scene!" George blurted out. "So, he was murdered."

"I think that's a safe assumption," Brie said, studying George and wondering if this was an act. She knew the shock of seeing someone murdered did odd things to people, denial being just one form the oddness took. But she'd also dealt with murderers who could have won an Academy Award for their performances.

"We'll talk to you at breakfast about what will be happening tomorrow," she said. "I'm sorry, but that's all I can tell you right now, except that I would like you all to lock your cabin doors."

This last comment created a murmur.

"Great, not only are we not sailing, but now there's a crazed maniac among us." Will's tone had shifted from snide to angry. "I think it's time to call the Coast Guard and get us off of this floating nightmare, Captain."

"I'm afraid that won't be possible, Will. I'll call them, but the Coast Guard will have their hands full with distress calls until the gale blows out."

"And this isn't distressing?" Will said, gesturing toward the body.

Tim spoke up. "The captain's right. They won't be coming unless there's an impending crisis."

DuLac turned to George. "Would you serve breakfast at 9:00 as planned? And could you make us some hot coffee before you go back to bed?"

"Aye, Captain." George glanced toward the body once more before heading down to the galley.

"Scott, you can go back to bed, but when Brie is finished up here, I'm going to call you to stand watch with me for the rest of the night. I'd like two people on deck until morning."

"Aye, Captain," Scott replied.

DuLac turned to Tim Pelletier next. "Tim, I'll need your help as well. Would you plan to be on deck at 6:30 AM.? We'll have to move the body, and possibly get it to shore if the Coast Guard can't get here."

"I'll be glad to help in any way I can, Captain," Tim answered.

"That's all for now," DuLac said. "I'll see you all at breakfast."

The passengers silently filed back to the companionways and disappeared down to their cabins. DuLac overheard Rob asking Alyssa, in a concerned way, if she was all right. Their voices drifted off before he could hear her reply.

Fortunately, Brie had grabbed her rain slicker when she dashed out of the cabin, but the wool socks on her feet were soaked from the water on the deck, and the cold was creeping up her body. DuLac was in bare feet, wearing a set of waterlogged sweats. And although the rain had slacked off temporarily, the wind coming

41

off the bluff above their anchorage chilled them through and through.

"You go below, Brie, and get into some dry clothes. I'll stay up here until you get back. George should have some fresh coffee for us soon."

Brie nodded. "I'll be back as quick as I can. I just need to get my camera and notebook. Would you ask George if he has some small paper bags and a few zipper baggies?"

"Sure," John responded.

"Oh, and do you, by chance, have any sort of magnifying glass?"

"I have one I use for chart reading. It's down in my cabin. I'll grab it."

"That'll be great." Brie turned and walked aft.

Down in her cabin, she peeled off the wet socks and pulled on a pair of dry jeans, followed by the pants to her foul-weather suit. She put on dry wool socks and slipped her feet into her rubber loafers. Then she clipped on her gun, grabbed her camera bag out of the corner and removed her Nikon and large flash. Winding off the roll of partially used film, she loaded on a new 24-exposure roll.

Next she pulled a small cosmetic case out of her duffel, located her tweezers and dropped them into her raincoat pocket. From her shoulder bag Brie retrieved a pocket tape recorder that she had started carrying after she was shot. One of the psychologists had suggested that she talk into it daily about what she was feeling. It was one of the things she had actually found helpful, so she'd kept on with it. She placed the recorder in her raincoat. She'd given up on the idea of a note pad when she heard the rain start again. Brie hung the camera around her neck, put on her raincoat and left the cabin.

As she emerged from the companionway and started forward, a violent gust of wind charged past her out to sea, threatening death to sailors in its path. DuLac was standing at the port rail near Pete's body. He turned as she approached, and in the lantern light she saw the hint of a tired smile.

"I feel responsible for this," he said.

"You're not, though," Brie said. "Sometimes bad things just happen, and much as we'd like to stop them, we can't."

He gripped the rail, staring into the darkness. "It goes with the territory of being a captain—you're responsible for everything aboard your ship."

Brie nodded, knowing how he felt. "I used to feel responsible every time my partner and I would get to a call too late and find someone dead. I had to learn how not to do that or the guilt would have crippled me—kept me from doing my job. It took a long time before I could separate my emotions from a crime scene. What you're experiencing is normal. Just give yourself some time to deal with all this. Okay?"

"I'll try," John said.

"You should go below now and get into some dry clothes. You'll feel better. I'll start photographing the scene." Brie removed the lens cap and slipped it into her pocket.

"I'm going to radio the Coast Guard about the murder. They'll need to pick up the body." But he knew with the seas out there, help wouldn't be arriving very soon. "Tim's right, if no one's in immediate danger, any distress call at sea will take precedence over ours. And having you aboard somewhat stabilizes the situation. Even though you're out of your jurisdiction, you're still a police officer."

John looked down at Pete's lifeless form. "I can't believe one of the people sleeping below deck right now could have done this. It scares me. What can we do to keep the others safe?"

"Aside from being watchful, I'm not sure. Being stuck aboard the ship in this remote place doesn't give us a lot of options. At least the killer can't escape; nowhere to go." She didn't speculate any further, but instead attached her flash to the camera and snapped off the first two shots.

George stuck his head out of the galley companionway.

"I have coffee, Captain, and here are those bags you wanted, Brie."

"Thanks, George," she said, setting them down in a dry corner.

"Just leave the coffee on the table down in the galley," DuLac said. "We'll get to it in awhile. You go back to bed now." He turned to Brie. "I'll be back up in a few minutes. Are you okay by yourself, or should George stay?"

"You go on, George. I'll be fine."

George headed back down to his berth.

"I need the flashlight left on the deck. Right there," Brie said, indicating the spot. "And don't worry, John. I'm wearing my gun."

John nodded thoughtfully. "I forgot about that. I'm glad you've got it with you."

"So, I'm fine, here," she said. "You go ahead and get changed." She understood his concerns, but she wanted to be alone. At this point she needed to carefully take in the details of the scene without distractions. She looked through the viewfinder, adjusted the lens to zoom in more tightly on the body, and snapped off two more shots.

Brie continued photographing the crime scene, moving around the body to cover all possible angles, taking a total of twenty-four close-up and slightly wider angle shots. She had just put the camera down in the galley when John arrived back on deck, wearing his rain gear. His face was grim.

"Well, we won't be calling the Coast Guard tonight. The radio transmitter's been tampered with. It's not working."

Brie looked surprised. "How can that be? The transmitter is in your cabin. You were sleeping when…"

John caught the look that barely registered on her face. "Unless I killed him— then taking out the radio would have been easy. Right?"

"Unfortunately, in a situation like this, everyone remains a suspect until they're cleared," Brie said uncomfortably. "But let's assume you didn't do it. What would the other possibilities be? How about during dinner, who was the last one down?"

"That would be me again," John said with a chuckle. "Things aren't looking good in my defense." He took a magnifying glass out of his pocket and handed it to her. "Here, you wanted this."

"Thanks," Brie said, putting it in a pocket. She picked up the flashlight and began carefully scanning the area around the body as she worked her way in toward it. "Scott and Pete both went up on deck when the fisherman came out. Scott was alone when Pete came down to get the money," she speculated. "But it was only for a couple of minutes."

"It doesn't take long to disable the radio if you know your way around it," John said. "Anyone on the crew could do it."

"Who was the last one on deck tonight when we found Pete?" Brie asked.

"Howard and Will arrived last, I think." DuLac was silent for a minute while he mulled over the possibilities. "I didn't go to my cabin right away when everyone retired last night. I talked to George in the galley for awhile as he made the coffee. I guess anyone could have slipped down there then."

"That would indicate premeditation," Brie said. She pulled the small recorder out of her pocket, turned it on and began recording a running commentary of the scene before her as she looked for clues. "Wednesday, May 14th, 3:45 AM. The victim is Peter McAllister, age 28, second mate aboard the schooner *Maine Wind*. The body was found at 3:15 AM. by Alyssa Lindstrom, a passenger. Condition of the body and color of the victim's skin indicate a time of death somewhere between 1:30 and 3:15 AM. The victim was stabbed with a marline spike—approximately ten inches in length. A rope wrapped around the victim's neck, as well as abrasions on the neck, indicate that the victim was strangled, and that the assailant attacked from behind." Brie bent closer to the body and, using the flashlight, inspected the abrasions on Pete's neck. Then she carefully took the rope from around his neck and placed it in one of the paper bags that George had provided. She folded the top over and put it in one of her large outer pockets. The rain started down again, hard, and with each gust of wind the ship creaked and groaned.

Brie worked her way meticulously over the body and the surrounding area. She was conscious of the captain watching her as she continued collecting evidence and recording her observations. Using her tweezers, she scraped slight traces of black fiber from under the fingernails on Pete's right hand into one of the baggies and zipped it closed. Inspecting the area closest to the body, she noticed a thick white rubber band lying near Pete's left hand.

"Do you know why this might be here?" she asked, illuminating it with the flashlight and looking up at John. The blustery conditions made it hard to communicate.

John squatted down. "It's a band used on lobsters' claws so they're safe to handle," he said over the wind. "Pete had dozens of them in all different colors. He'd devised this method of weaving them into things."

"Of course. I saw him doing that on deck one night and asked him about it. He said it was just an odd hobby he'd invented to pass the time, since he didn't much like reading and didn't play an instrument like Scott."

"That one must have fallen out of his pocket in the struggle," John speculated. "Or he may have been playing with it when he was attacked."

Brie felt in Pete's raincoat pocket and discovered a stash of lobster bands. She picked up the one on deck with her tweezers, bagged it, and dropped it into her pocket. She continued her painstaking inspection of the body and its surroundings for another fifteen minutes. When she was satisfied that she had recorded all her observations and collected any evidence present, she turned to John.

"We can cover him now. I'll check for evidence underneath the body when we move it in the morning. Do you have a tarp on board?"

"Down in the storeroom. I'll go get it."

John was back up in a couple of minutes with the tarp. He helped Brie drape it over the body and tuck it securely underneath so the wind wouldn't blow it off.

"That should work for the next couple of hours," he said, standing up and stepping back. There was a moment of awkward silence as they stood over Pete's corpse. At length John murmured, "Lord, bring him to a safe and peaceful rest."

"Amen," Brie murmured.

As they turned away, John put an arm behind Brie. "I could stand some coffee," he said, looking down at her. "Will you join me?"

"Sure," said Brie. "It'll feel good to get out of this wind and rain."

They descended to the galley, where George had left a kerosene lamp burning and a carafe of coffee on the table with two mugs. Alongside was a plate covered in plastic wrap with what looked like banana bread on it.

Brie collapsed onto one of the benches behind the table. She felt the familiar pressure of the holstered gun at her side, but it offered little reassurance. After all, it hadn't saved Phil. DuLac pulled a short wooden stool out of the galley and sat across from her. They both reached for the mugs, and John poured out coffee for both of them. With a tired gesture Brie pushed the hood off her head and leaned back against the ship's hull. She wrapped her hands around the warm mug. A shiver ran through her, as much from the crime scene she'd been poring over for an hour as from the effect of the mug on her cold hands.

"I can't imagine doing that kind of work for long without burning out." John took a large gulp from his mug as he studied her. "Is that why you took a leave?"

He watched a shadow pass over Brie's lovely eyes. When she started to speak, there was a hollowness in her voice.

"My partner and I were heading back from a crime scene one

night. An intruder call came across the radio. We were nearby, so we responded. We entered the house. He came out of nowhere. Phil lunged in front of me. Took the bullet." Her sentences came in short bursts like gasps for air. "I woke in the hospital. The bullet had passed through Phil, killing him, and lodged in my left side—an inch from my heart."

John saw the torment in her eyes.

"It should have been me. Phil had a wife and a young son. I had no one." Brie looked at her coffee, unable to lift it, her arms weighted down by her words.

John spoke quietly. "The instinct to save another is very strong in good people." He reached out and took her hand, hoping to bring her back from that dark place.

The *Maine Wind* creaked in the silence.

"After I healed up, I went back on duty. Thought I could work through my anxiety. Then the dreams started, and I began reliving that night more often. So I got counseling. They told me it was post-traumatic stress disorder—you know, like the soldiers get. They gave me lots of strategies for dealing with the panic attacks, but none of it worked very well. So, I took a leave. The irony of all this is that I came to Maine, to the sea, to get as far away from my work as possible. Hopefully gain a new perspective. And here I am again, in the thick of it."

"Unfortunately, evil never takes a leave."

"Most people think of my work in the field of criminology as something dark and macabre." She looked down at her hands on the mug. "It's not, entirely."

John watched her for a moment. "Revealing the truth…it's noble work, Brie."

Brie looked up at him. She'd almost forgotten why she had chosen her occupation. "Thank you for that," she said. But behind her words something stirred. It felt like hope.

John reached for the plate George had left on the table. "I think George is depending on us to make this bread do a disappearing act." Uncovering the plate, he took a piece. "I wouldn't want to disappoint him."

"Me either." Brie smiled as she reached for the plate.

"It's 4:45," said John. "You should try to get a little more sleep before 6:30 rolls around. I have a feeling tomorrow's going to be a long day."

"The first thing is to get the body to shore." Brie brushed a crumb from her mouth. "Do you know if anyone on the island has a place where it could be stored?" she asked. "Maybe a large cooler?"

"Fred Klemper runs the general store. He's got a cooler. We'll go there first."

"Then we need to radio the Coast Guard. Is there any form of law enforcement on the island?" Brie asked. "Maybe a sheriff or town constable?"

"I'm not sure if there is on Granite Island. Judging from the size of the community, I'm guessing there won't be. But Fred will know."

"It might be good to follow through with your idea of visiting the inn tomorrow. A hot shower would be wonderful, and it would get people off the boat. The inn also might provide a little more privacy for me to start questioning the passengers. I guess it would depend on how well you know the owners, though. After what's happened tonight, they may not be comfortable having us there, even though I'm a police officer."

"Glenn and Betty Johnson own Snug Harbor. They're close friends of Ben Rutledge—my friend I mentioned this afternoon. My father died when I was 16. His death left me a confused, angry and withdrawn kid. Ben took me under his wing, taught me about sailing, the sea, and many more important things. That was how I came to the *Maine Wind*. She was his ship. When he wanted to retire from the cruising business, I took her over. Glenn and Betty are a lot like him. They're just good people—salt of the earth. I know they'll help in any way they can."

John paused, slowly rotating the cup in his hands.

"What is it, John?"

"Do you…" He hesitated. "Do you think the rest of us are in danger?"

"It's hard to say. I wish I could tell you we're not, but I can't. I do know that most murderers have one motive and are after one victim. The only constant is that they're desperate people. The person in danger is the one who gets too close to the truth."

"And that would be you," John said bluntly.

"Yup."

"I won't let anything happen to you. I promise."

He said it with such force in his voice and such intensity in his eyes that Brie felt instantly safe. As a detective she knew she was still vulnerable, but the woman in her felt shielded by his determination. Reluctantly she reminded herself that John was still a suspect. She couldn't eliminate him just because he made her feel safe.

"I just remembered. Glenn is a ham radio operator," John said. "He'll be able to radio the Coast Guard. We'll stop up at the inn and talk to him and Betty after we leave the body at Fred's store. We'll decide then whether to bring people ashore."

Brie yawned wide. Exhaustion had hit. "Maybe I *will* try to catch another hour or so of sleep if it's okay with you."

"I want you to."

Brie stood up. "Then I'll see you at 6:30." In what had in recent months become an uncharacteristic gesture, she reached out and laid her hand on his. "I'm sorry about this, John."

"Me too," he said, getting up. "I'll walk you to your cabin."

With John behind her, Brie climbed the ladder and headed aft, surveying the body as she passed, making sure the tarp was secure. They descended the ladder to her cabin. John opened the door, flipped on the light and scanned the small quarters.

"All clear," he said.

"Thanks," said Brie, aware of the irony in this situation. A little more than a year ago this kind of behavior from a man would have turned her off. Now, she felt oddly grateful.

She stepped into her cabin and locked the door. Her nerves felt raw. Trouble had followed her—she hadn't escaped it. The thought of a murder invading her vacation made her angry. *Vacation*? She chuckled at the thought. You *plan* a vacation. One day she'd thrown together a duffel full of clothes and called the head of the department to tell him that she was taking the leave he'd offered her. She'd taken a cab to the airport, cleared the gun paperwork, and found a seat on a plane bound for Detroit with a connecting flight to Maine. The whole thing had taken three hours. That wasn't planning—that was running.

Her sleeping bag beckoned. Peeling off her rain gear, she hung it on the back of the door. She exchanged her jeans for a pair of cozy sweatpants and crawled into bed. She set her small travel alarm for 6:15 and tucked it under her pillow, along with her gun. Then, closing her eyes, she took some deep breaths and lay there for a few minutes using a mental technique she'd developed for turning off her thoughts. Phil moved in front of her, taking the bullet, then he was gone. The rain beat on the deck above her in a steady rhythm. Sleep finally came.

5

BRIE WOKE AT 6:10, pulled her clock out from under the pillow and turned off the alarm. She stretched in her bag, unleashing a series of pops along her spine, then reached up and massaged her scalp to wake herself up. Previews of the day's responsibilities began to race through her mind. For all intents and purposes, her vacation was over. Today she'd be questioning the passengers and crew—hoping to flush out a killer. The possibility of that sent a shiver through her. She was used to working as part of a team on homicides. But until the Coast Guard could get to them, she was *it*. John would back her up, of course, but she was the one with the experience and the gun.

Yesterday, in the storm, the ship had felt like a safe haven. What a difference a day could make. With a sudden twinge of homesickness, Brie thought about her apartment back in Minneapolis. Her mom had always chided her about being a minimalist. It was true—except for a few cozy afghans and too many books, her small Minneapolis apartment was fairly spartan. Brie also had mixed feelings about technology and, in her private life, clung to an almost anachronistic simplicity. The psychiatrist in her had long ago recognized this tendency as an attempt to create some balance with her emotionally complex job. Anyway, as far as she was concerned, less stuff meant more time. She had used that time to advance her career. But she wondered now, as she lay in her berth, whether that had been the wisest choice.

After a minute or two, Brie dammed up her stream of consciousness and unzipped her sleeping bag. She sat up and dangled her legs over the edge of the berth. The cabin was cold and damp. A metallic taste in her mouth told her she hadn't had enough sleep. She grabbed her toothbrush and filled her cup from the wooden cask. The strong taste of mint started to bring her around. After rinsing her mouth, she ran the hairbrush through her hair eight or ten times, her scalp tingling under the bristles, and then pulled the hair back into a ponytail. She exchanged the sweat pants she'd slept in for a pair of jeans, pulled on a grey wool sweater that matched her mood, and went to use the head at the end of the passageway.

The nor'easter was still making its presence known, and rain drummed persistently on the cabin top above her. Great day to move a body, she thought, glancing upward. In a few minutes Brie was back in her cabin. She clipped on her gun, put on her foul-weather gear and rubber loafers, and headed topside.

The captain was standing up near the bow with George, who disappeared down the galley companionway as she approached.

"Hey, Brie. Were you able to sleep?"

"Yup. But considering how I felt when I woke up, I might have been better off just staying up."

George came back on deck and handed her a steaming mug of coffee. "Morning, Brie."

"Thanks, George. Your coffee makes standing in this rain almost tolerable. I thought you'd take the chance to sleep in this morning since breakfast is later than usual."

George shrugged. "I'm best if I stick to my schedule. Creature

53

of habit, I guess. So, what's the plan, Captain?" As George spoke, Scott and Tim came on deck wearing their foul-weather gear.

"Morning, gentlemen," the captain greeted them. "We'll get started right away if that's all right. George, you may as well stick around for a couple minutes. We may need your help." He turned to Scott. "Would you bring up the backboard from the storeroom? We'll use it as a stretcher. And grab a roll of duct tape."

"Aye, Captain."

"We'll place the tarp underneath the body when we move it onto the backboard," DuLac said. "Then we'll tape the tarp closed and lash the body to the board so we can lower it to the yawl boat."

Brie spoke up. "What you'll see under the tarp will be shocking —I want you to be prepared."

The five of them moved over to the body. But despite Brie's warning, as they uncovered it George stepped back in shock.

"Jesus!"

The bluish tinge of Pete's skin was amplified by the yellow of his rain gear, and rigor mortis had set in, hardening his features into a grotesque mask.

The four men lifted the body onto the backboard and wrapped the tarp around it. They taped and lashed it. Then, with each man taking a corner of the board, they made their way to the stern of the ship.

Brie checked the area under the body to make sure she hadn't missed any evidence. She stooped down and inspected the deck planking where Pete's head had been. Taking the tweezers from her pocket she removed several wavy blond hairs caught between the planks. She placed them in a baggie, zipped it up and dropped it into her pocket to add to the other evidence.

Scott and Tim went over the stern and down the ladder to the yawl boat while the captain attached one of the pulleys to the lashings around the body. Then, he and George hoisted it up and slowly lowered it down to Scott and Tim. Once the body was secured, John and Brie climbed down to the boat.

"We'll try to be back by breakfast," he called up to George.

With that Scott turned over the engine and released the line that secured them to the *Maine Wind*. It was almost seven o'clock as he steered the yawl boat over the choppy water of the bay toward the waterfront docks of the village.

"Once we land, I'll go up to the general store and rouse Fred Klemper," John said. "The rest of you can wait in the boat. No point taking the body out until we know where we're going with it."

As they crossed the cove, Brie studied the village for signs of life. Except for the smoke that curled from a few chimneys, she found none. The small harbor was dotted with lobsterboats bobbing at their moorings. No fishermen would be heading out today. Yesterday's gale had become a full-blown nor'easter, packing high winds and piling up huge seas.

Crowning the bluff above the village was a large white Victorian house with cranberry-colored shutters and a porch running around three sides of it.

As if reading her mind, John pointed toward it. "That's Snug Harbor Bed and Breakfast."

"They must have some view from up there," Brie said.

As they got closer to shore, Scott slowed the yawl boat to an idle and they floated the last few yards up to the dock. John threw the bow-line over a piling, hopped onto the dock and secured the stern line that Scott threw him.

"I'll be back in a few minutes," he said. He turned and strode off the dock and up a small hill toward the general store. Brie, Scott and Tim waited with the body.

John was back in fifteen minutes. "Fred says we can put the body in his cooler until the Coast Guard gets here. He told me that over the years he's had occasion to store two other bodies in the cooler when people died suddenly and there was no way to get them to the mainland." John gave Brie a hand up out of the yawl boat.

"Did you ask him if there's a constable on the island?" Brie asked.

"Fred said there isn't. So, for now at least, we're on our own."

Brie looked out to sea. There was no horizon line, only a grayness that seemed to match the lack of definition she felt. When she turned back there was resignation in her voice. "I guess this means I'll be conducting the investigation by myself," she said. "So, let's get the body to a secure place, and then we need to get to a radio."

"Scott, you and Tim lift the backboard up. Brie and I'll help slide it onto the dock." This done, Scott and Tim boosted themselves out of the boat, and, with each person on a corner, they started for the general store with the body.

As they made their way along, Brie scanned the cluster of houses that huddled along the hill near the waterfront. From the second-story window of a small Cape-Cod house, a woman with raven hair watched them. When she realized Brie had noticed her, she stepped back into the shadows. Brie wasn't surprised. In a tiny village like this she imagined lots of other windows were occupied by curious onlookers. *I'd certainly be interested if I saw four people carrying what looked like a body through the rain.*

When they arrived at the back door of his store, Fred Klemper was waiting for them. He was a ghost of a man, tall, thin and anemic looking. Ideal to watch over a corpse, Brie thought. She had the odd impression that, were he placed in front of a bright light, she'd see right through him. The magnifying glasses he wore slid down his nose, and with a spindly finger he pushed them back up. Brie noticed a gleam of anticipation in his owlish eyes, as if he relished the thought of a murder victim in his cooler. She could picture him creeping in there late at night for a peek, to add a little excitement to what she suspected was an existence lacking in drama.

They followed Fred through the back door into a storeroom that held a small walk-in cooler.

Fred preceded them into the cooler and gestured to the right. "You can put him against the wall there," he said. "I've moved all the food to the other side."

They maneuvered the body through the door. As they entered the cooler, Brie noted that the temperature on the large ther-mometer was just above freezing—perfectly suited to their needs. They placed Pete's body along the right wall and quickly exited the makeshift morgue.

John introduced his crew and then struck up a brief conver-sation with Fred. "I'm hoping the Coast Guard will be able to get to us by tomorrow or the day after," he said. "We certainly appre-ciate your help, Fred."

"No problem. Glad to be of help. Storm's pretty bad. May be a few days." Fred spoke in a slow cadence, punctuating each state-ment with a series of either nods or shakes of his head—an eccen-tricity that amused Brie.

"He'll be safe in here," Fred continued. "I always lock the cooler at night."

John suppressed a smile. We wouldn't want the body to make a break for it, he thought to himself.

"Well, thanks again, Fred, we'll get out of your way now."

"Would you like some coffee? Just gonna make some." Fred glanced across the storeroom to where he kept a coffee maker next to his old roll-top desk.

"Thanks, but we have to stop up at the inn and then get back to the ship," John shook Fred's thin hand carefully. "I'll take a rain check, though."

"Sure enough." Fred got off two nods. "There'll be plenty of rain for usin' that check the next few days," he said with enthusiasm, as if the prospect of more rain were cause for excessive glee.

They left by the back door and headed around the side of the store to the gravel road that wound past the village and up toward Snug Harbor Bed and Breakfast. Mud sucked at their shoes as they slogged along. Brie was glad for the exercise. It kept the cold at bay and helped to relieve some of the stress that had been building inside her since Alyssa's middle-of-the-night scream.

She fell into step with John. "How old are Glenn and Betty?" she asked

"I think they're around 65," John said. "I know they're close to Ben's age, and he's 68."

"We need to tell Glenn to have the Coast Guard contact the authorities where Pete lived, so his family will be notified."

"I brought along Pete's application to give Glenn. It has his parents' address and phone number on it. They live in Brunswick. I'm planning to visit them when we get back to the mainland."

A few more minutes' climb brought them around the last curve in the road, and there stood the inn. Brie stopped to take in the setting. Even with rain falling, the place had such appeal. Stately cedar trees graced the sloping lawn, and wild rose bushes that Glenn had transplanted from around the island grew along the base of the porch. Comfortable wicker furniture and wooden rocking chairs invited guests to sit and take in the view of the cove below and the ocean beyond.

They made their way across the wide lawn and climbed the porch steps. Brie turned and looked out to sea. "A place like this could make you look forward to retirement," she said.

John stepped onto the porch directly behind her. "That view sure is easy on the soul." He suddenly had an urge to slip his arms around her and close the gap between them; he could almost feel her head resting on his shoulder. Had circumstances been different, he might have followed through.

The door of the inn opened and Betty stepped out. "John, is that you? We saw the *Maine Wind* in the cove."

John walked over and gave her a big hug. "Hello, Betty. It's good to see you again."

"How are you, dear?" she said, with all the warmth of a mother to her own son.

"I'm fine, just fine. I apologize for the hour."

"Oh, nonsense! Glenn and I are always up at the crack of dawn. Come in, come in. It's nasty out here." She ushered them through the front door into a wide hallway.

A pumpkin-pine floor glowing with orange and brown tones stretched toward a formal staircase that ascended to the second floor. A jade-green oriental rug filled the center of the hall. On it sat a heavy-hewn table and on the table, a rustic pitcher filled with lilacs.

"Glenn!" Betty called. "It's John. John is here."

"Well, for heaven sakes," Glenn said as he came out of the library at the back of the central hallway. He was wearing his slippers and reading glasses, but that was as far as the old man image went. He came across the hall with the stride of a man in his forties and gave John a backslapping hug. "How are you, son?"

"Just fine, Glenn. You're looking as spry as ever."

"That's thanks to Betty. She doesn't let me get too lazy. And who are these fine folks?"

"These are two of my shipmates, Brie Beaumont and Tim Pelletier," John said. "And this is Scott Hogan, my first mate."

"Come and have some coffee. And tell us what brings you up here so early," Betty said. They removed their shoes, and Betty herded them back toward the kitchen.

"Actually, Brie and I need to speak to you and Glenn privately," John said. "Maybe Scott and Tim could wait in the kitchen."

"That's fine. Let me get you all some coffee. Then we'll go into the living room."

They moved through the second door on the left into a formal dining room.

"Wow, this is lovely." Brie was surprised by the amount of light pouring into the room on such a dreary day. On the opposite wall a long bank of leaded-glass windows looked out onto an ornately fenced perennial garden. "This must be incredible on a sunny day," she said.

They walked through the dining room and into the inn's large kitchen. Brie looked around. The room was a good fifteen feet wide and ran all the way across the back of the inn. A sturdy worktable with a butcher-block top sat in the center of the kitchen, and at the far end were three, square tables covered with gingham cloths, each with a set of high-back chairs around it. Brie could imagine the guests gathering here for coffee and conversation. As they hung their raincoats on the chairs, Glenn noticed Brie's gun and sent John a concerned look.

Betty moved over to the cupboard next to the stove and took out six stoneware mugs. She filled them with steaming coffee and handed two of them to Scott and Tim. "Now, you two gentlemen make yourselves at home," she said. From the back of the counter she brought out a plate of cranberry muffins, removed the plastic wrap and set them on the work table. "Help yourselves. You must be hungry."

"Thanks, Betty. That's very kind," John said. "We could all use a few calories about now." He and Brie selected muffins and placed them on the plates Betty had set out. Then they took their mugs of coffee and walked into the living room with Glenn and Betty. They sat in four wing chairs that flanked a brown brick fireplace.

John wasted no time broaching the topic. "I'm sorry to tell you this, but it's a grim situation that brings us here. Last night my second mate, Pete McAllister, was murdered on board the *Maine Wind*."

"Lord save us!" Betty's hands flew up to cover her mouth. Glenn jumped up and stepped over behind her chair. He placed his hands comfortingly on her shoulders. Betty seemed suddenly older and frailer.

Silence fell—the aftershock of what had been revealed. Finally Glenn spoke. "What can we do to help you, John?"

"First of all, our radio was sabotaged, and we need to notify the Coast Guard."

"I'll radio them immediately," Glenn said. "What else can we do?"

"It so happens that Brie is a detective, on leave from the Minneapolis Police Department."

"That's amazing too," Glenn said. "What are the chances of that?" He glanced at her gun—this time with relief.

John continued. "Our problem is, with the storm blowing, we could be stuck here for several days. And considering what's happened, I think it would be good to get the passengers off the ship for a while. I was hoping we might bring them here for the day. Brie needs to begin questioning them, and the inn would offer more privacy for doing that."

"You're certainly welcome to use the inn, John," Betty said.

Glenn hesitated as he looked down at Betty. "Are you concerned for the safety of any of the other passengers?" he asked.

"It's the most important consideration in a situation like this," said Brie. "We must take every precaution. As I've explained to John, most murderers are after one victim, but the fact is, we just don't know. Frankly, I'd feel better if you and Betty weren't here if we bring the others to the inn. But would you be comfortable having us here when you're gone?"

"We trust John," Glenn said. He turned to face DuLac. "You know your way around this place as well as anyone; I know you won't let anything bad happen here. You and Ben have certainly helped us out enough over the years. This would give us a chance to return a little of your kindness. I'll leave it to Betty to arrange the details with you. I'd like to get that call in to the Coast Guard."

John gave Glenn the sheet containing Pete's information and asked him to have the Coast Guard notify the authorities in Brunswick.

"Do you have any friends on the island you might visit for the day?" Brie asked Betty.

"We could probably visit our friends, Frank and Helen Thompson, who live on the other side of the island. They've wanted us to stop over and help them plan some new garden space. Glenn is quite a gardener, you know." As she spoke, Betty made a motion with her hand, indicating the perennial garden on the west side of the inn. "I'll give them a call right now, if you'll excuse me."

"John and I'll wait here," Brie said.

Betty headed for the door to the hallway, but before leaving the room, she paused and turned back to them. "You know there's something familiar about that name—Pete's name. I just can't seem to remember why." Shaking her head in a distracted way, she turned and left the room.

John sat back down, and he and Brie took the opportunity to eat their muffins and down their mugs of coffee.

Glenn came back into the room first. "I reached the Coast Guard and reported the situation. They said they're swamped with distress calls from the gale and if no one's in immediate danger, they'll get to you after the storm has lessened. Sounds like it could be at least another twenty-four hours."

"I expected as much," John said.

"Oh, and they'll notify the police over in Brunswick to get hold of Pete's parents."

"Thanks, Glenn."

"Betty went to call your friends, the Thompsons. She thought you two might spend the day with them," Brie said.

"That's perfect," Glenn nodded. "We've been planning to get over to their place for two months now. So, in a way you've done us a favor. Be watchful of things, though, John. Betty and I have put our hearts into Snug Harbor. We'd hate to have anything compromise our feelings for this place."

"I'll make sure nothing happens, Glenn. Before I forget, is it all right if the passengers use your extra shower facilities downstairs? Before all this happened, I promised if we came up here they could all get a nice hot shower."

"By all means," Glenn said, "and, what's more, it's on the house." He turned to Brie to explain. "Part of what we advertise is that boaters are always welcome to stop at the inn for a hot shower and a hot lunch. We installed some nice facilities downstairs. There are five shower stalls with a small dressing room off each. We supply towels and hair dryers for a fee of $5.00 per shower. It's surprising how many people we get—I guess the shower facilities on most boats aren't all that great. Quite a few folks who come up for a shower end up staying for either lunch or tea. So, it's a nice little sideline business. And a good number of them have returned at some point to stay at the inn."

Betty came back in. "We're all set with the Thompsons," she said. "They invited us to stay for dinner, too. John, would you like me to prepare a lunch for your passengers before we leave?" she asked.

"No need for that, Betty. Our cook, George Dupopolis, will take care of preparing lunch if you don't mind him using the kitchen."

"Heavens no," Betty said, waving a hand. "Tell him to help himself to whatever he needs. There are plenty of supplies in the larder."

"We'll have dinner back on the ship later in the evening," John said, standing up. "We should start back. It's 8:00, and I was hoping to get back to the ship by 8:15." He and Brie picked up their plates and mugs. As the four of them walked back to the kitchen, Glenn gave John a key to the inn, along with a phone number where he and Betty could be reached.

"Thanks again, you two. I'll lock up when we leave this evening, and Brie and I will stop back up here before the *Maine Wind* leaves its anchorage."

"Good luck, and stay safe," Glenn said.

They rounded up Scott and Tim, and after donning their raincoats, the four of them headed for the front door. They waved goodbye to Betty and Glenn as they descended the porch stairs.

A cold northeast wind blowing over the top of the island assaulted them as they emerged from the shelter of the inn and crossed the front lawn. Storm clouds roiled overhead. It felt good to Brie to drop down along the road, out of the biting wind, toward the cove. She thought about why Pete's name might have seemed familiar to Betty. Could he have stayed at the inn? As she surveyed the *Maine Wind* lying at anchor, its masts, like skeleton fingers, pointed accusingly at the ominous sky, she wondered what other dark surprises this day had in store.

6

AS THE YAWL BOAT CROSSED the harbor, Brie watched the *Maine Wind* for signs of life but found none. The passengers were either sleeping in or clinging to their cabins to stay out of the raw weather until George rang the breakfast bell calling them down to the galley. They approached the stern of the ship, with Scott cutting the engine a few yards away. Brie noticed Scott had been unusually silent this morning, engaging in none of the easy banter she'd come to identify with him. He helped DuLac secure the yawl boat to the stern of the ship, and the four of them climbed the ladder with Brie leading the way.

"Thanks for your help, Tim," DuLac said.

"Glad to," Tim replied. "If there's nothing else you need right now, I'd like to go below and wash up before breakfast."

"Go ahead," DuLac said. "Scott, let's tighten up those lashings around the mainsail."

Brie caught his arm as he started to hop up on top of the cabin. "Captain, I need to ask you some questions before we take the passengers ashore this morning. You have important background information on the crew, and possibly a few facts about some of the others that may be of help. I'd like to get that information from you now, because once we get to the inn, I'll need you to keep an eye on everyone while I'm doing the questioning."

"That's fine, Brie. Just tell me when and where."

"We need to talk someplace private."

"How about my cabin, before breakfast? We still have a half hour."

"What about Rob and Alyssa?" Brie asked. "Their cabin is just across the passageway."

"I'll go down right now and ask if they could go forward to the galley early.

"Great. I'll help Scott finish up on deck and meet you down there in a few minutes."

Having secured the sail, Scott hopped down off the cabin top. "Brie, could you help me bring the kerosene lanterns down to the storeroom?" he asked.

"Sure, I'll get the ones up near the bow and bring them below."

Moving forward, Brie retrieved a lamp hanging from the ratlines—a ladder-like system of rods and rope, used for going aloft, that ran at an angle from the sides of the ship, three quarters of the way up the masts. Over the last three days, she had watched the crew climb the ratlines to work on the topsails and rigging far above the deck. They reminded her of trapeze artists and tightrope walkers at the circus, climbing to their tiny perches above the audience. The sailor in her longed to climb up there. She'd have to get John's permission to do it before they got back to the mainland.

She found a second lamp on the galley cabin top and started down to the storeroom. At the bottom of the ladder she nearly collided with Tim, who was pulling a white tee-shirt over his head as he headed for the bathroom. She took in the unusual tattoo on his chest. It depicted either a rising or a setting sun, and there was a woman's name under it. Brie wondered if it implied that the sun both rose and set in this woman. She thought back to their conversation at dinner last night; he hadn't mentioned a girlfriend. She made a mental note to ask him about it when she questioned him.

Proceeding into the storeroom, she placed the lanterns in their cabinet, and passed Scott on her way out the door. "See you at breakfast," she said. She headed to the stern of the ship for her meeting with the captain. At the bottom of the companionway ladder she rapped on the door to her left.

"All clear down here?" she asked when John opened his door.

"Yup," he replied. "Rob and Alyssa jumped at the chance for an early cup of coffee in the galley. They both looked like hell. Alyssa had obviously been crying a lot, and Rob looked like he could use a strong drink—and I'm not talking coffee."

"I need to grab my recorder and notepad in my cabin, and we'll get started," Brie said.

She was back a few moments later. Stepping into DuLac's cabin, she closed the door after her and looked around. On the back wall was a chart table and, under the table, a wood rack with small, square pigeonholes that held rolled-up charts of all the coastal waters John sailed. A bookcase next to the table was filled with books on sailing and the sea. Directly across from the door was a double berth, half of which tucked under the deck overhead, and just to the left of the door was the radio transmitter—now inoperable. In front of the chart table was a wooden chair, the seat of which both swiveled and rocked. Brie noticed it was bolted to the floorboards so it wouldn't fly around when the ship was under sail. John rocked back in the chair, hands locked behind his head, one foot propped on his knee. He wore a red flannel shirt that set off his dark hair and placed a butterfly in Brie's chest.

"Would you like the chair, Brie? I can sit on the berth," he said, starting to get up.

"That's okay. I'll just sit up here."

Climbing onto the berth, Brie folded her legs under her Indian style. Her detective training had taught her to position herself higher than the person being questioned, thus creating the psychological sense of having the upper hand. She wasn't sure, though, if having the upper hand by sitting on the bed of a man you were attracted to, who was, coincidentally, a suspect, would qualify as correct procedure. But what the heck, it was the best she could do.

Brie switched on the recorder and began to speak. "Wednesday, May 14th. Interview with John DuLac, captain of the schooner *Maine Wind*." She rewound a little of the tape to make sure it was recording and then addressed John.

"I'll start with some questions about Pete, and then move on to some background on Scott and George," she said.

"Okay, shoot."

"How long have you known Pete McAllister?"

"Only since March, when I hired him to crew this summer."

"Do you know who employed him previously?"

"He was second mate on the *Yankee Pride*. Jim Gallaway is the skipper. I checked with him before I hired Pete."

"And what did you find out about his time on that ship?" Brie asked.

"Jim said he was a hard worker and excellent on the high rigging, which was one of the main reasons I hired him. The first and second mates frequently have to go up the masts to do a repair or unfoul a line or sail while we're under way. You want the most sure-footed mate you can get at the top of a swaying 80-foot mast. Pete was made for that work. He was a rock climber—had even taught some classes in it, I hear. He had absolutely no fear up there."

"You admired him," Brie said.

"There are aspects of sailing that require raw courage. Pete had it, and I admired that part of him."

Brie wondered, recalling Pete's face in the midst of the gale yesterday. She knew that the real test of courage often comes when you're face to face with something gravely beyond your control—when you're hurled blind into the darkness.

"Don't get me wrong," John said, as if reading her doubts. "Pete had his flaws like all of us."

"And what were those?" Brie asked.

"Pete liked the ladies, and sometimes he didn't discriminate between the married and unmarried ones. It got him in trouble on the *Yankee Pride*. Jim Gallaway warned me about it. You saw the result of his outrageous flirting last night at dinner. I thought Rob Lindstrom might kill him on the spot. I warned Pete before I turned in—any more of that and he wouldn't finish the season with me."

"Did Jim Gallaway fire him?"

"No. Jim's long-time second mate had been injured a few weeks before the season began last year. When he hired Pete, Jim made it clear that it was only for one season."

"Did you hear anything unusual in the night? Anything wake you?" Brie asked.

"If it had I'd have been up on deck moments later. It's my job to check out anything I hear. A ship lying at anchor is always vulnerable. That's why we stand watch. Everyone on the crew is trained to respond to any unusual noise or vibration. Unfortunately, I heard nothing. Yesterday was an exhausting day, and I was out like a light the minute I hit my bunk."

John studied Brie as she jotted down notes. He hoped this interview would take a while. He liked Brie sitting on his bed and wished he could be over there with her. He had become increasingly attracted to her over the last few days and found her straightforward, no-nonsense demeanor refreshing. She displayed a kind of bare-bones honesty that was a rare find in anyone, man or woman. To top it off, he found her simply beautiful, with the emphasis on simple. Everything about her suggested clean straight lines, from her perfect posture to her long blonde hair.

She had the kind of translucent beauty that needed no make-up or fancy clothing to enhance it. He guessed she had been an athlete at one time; there was a refined strength about her movements that implied some form of disciplined physical training. But she was also somewhat of a study in contrasts, he thought. Strength mixed with vulnerability, self-assurance coupled with shyness. She was complex, and in that lay a challenge. John liked challenges.

"John?" Brie looked at him quizzically. She checked her watch, eager to finish questioning him.

"Sorry. What was the question again?" he asked, flustered. "I was just thinking about something."

Brie smiled. "Anything you'd like to share?"

"No. I mean, not right now," he fumbled. "It doesn't relate to the murder."

"Well then, the question was, did either Scott or George know Pete before he came to work on the *Maine Wind*?"

"I'm sure that Scott and George had heard his name—the names of crew members within the fleet tend to get around, but I think they met Pete for the first time a few weeks ago, when we all got together to go over plans for this season."

"Did they both seem to get along with him?" Brie asked.

"You've seen about as much of that interaction as I have. We've only been working together for two weeks. Pete was easy enough to like, though. He had a positive outlook on life."

"Can you think of anyone else on board who might have had a grudge against him?"

"Will Thackeray also applied for the second mate's job this season and was mighty upset he didn't get it."

"Really! Well, that explains his antagonism toward Pete."

"Will came up here in March looking for a job on one of the windjammers. He graduated college this spring, and I think he saw the windjammer job as kind of one last fling before joining the adult world."

"But you didn't hire him."

"Will had plenty of sailing experience—more than Pete actually—but I decided on Pete because he'd crewed aboard another windjammer. I guess I felt a little bad about Will, so I offered him a fifty percent discount if he wanted to come on the first cruise. You don't think he had anything to do with Pete's death, do you? I mean, people don't kill each other over summer jobs."

"People will kill each other over just about anything you can imagine."

"But you'd have to be completely unbalanced to kill someone over a summer job."

Brie gave him a wry smile. "Murderers generally are unbalanced," she said. "So, anything else you can think of that might point to a motive?"

"You mean other than Rob with his insane jealousy, which Alyssa seems to take great pleasure in aggravating? That outburst last night was right on the edge. If he caught those two together again, I don't know what he might have done."

"Well, one thing's for certain," Brie said, "one of these people had a compelling reason to do away with Pete. When we get to the inn, I'll call a friend of mine back at the department and have him run the names of everyone on board through NCIC to see if anything comes up. I'll also have him check their home towns. At least we'll know if anyone on board has a prior offense. So, if you have addresses for all the passengers and crew I'll jot them down. I'll also need their birth dates, but I can get those at breakfast."

"Does that include me?" John asked, reaching into the drawer under the chart table and pulling out two manila folders containing information on the passengers and crew.

"I'm afraid it does," Brie said, feeling uncomfortable—and feeling bothered that she felt uncomfortable.

He stood up and came over to her with the files. "I suppose now you'll find out I used to be the mad bomber, and I won't stand a chance with you."

Brie tried but failed to suppress her laugh. "You never know, it might make for some explosive chemistry." She locked eyes with him momentarily as she reached for the files, and electricity filled the gap between them. At that moment the breakfast bell rang, short-circuiting the connection. Brie hopped off the berth. Saved by the bell, she thought to herself. What was she doing making a comment like that? Her life was complicated enough right now without adding John DuLac to the pile. She reminded herself that she lived in Minnesota and would have to go back there sooner or later. She headed for the door, trying not to look at him.

"By the way, you won't find me in those files, but I was born and raised in Bath, Maine, and now live near Camden."

Remembering something, she turned around. "I need your permission to search the passengers' cabins while they're at breakfast."

"You've got it. Since the cabins only lock from the inside, you'll be able to get into all of them, now that everyone has gone forward for breakfast."

"Maybe you could tell them I'm going over some notes and that I'll be down in a few minutes."

"No problem. I'll make sure no one leaves the galley."

"Great! See you in a little bit." Brie stepped out the door and into her cabin to drop off the files. She lingered there, still flustered by what was obviously a mutual attraction between her and John. When she came back out a couple minutes later, she was glad to see he'd gone to breakfast.

7

BRIE WALKED ACROSS THE PASSAGEWAY and stepped into Rob and Alyssa's cabin. She was looking for anything that might connect one of the people aboard to the crime scene or personally to Pete. On the floor by the wall were two duffels containing their clothes and personal items. She lifted them up on the berth and started looking through the first one. There were three things Brie knew definitely about the crime. First, the murderer was right-handed, indicated by the angle at which the marline spike was driven into Pete's chest. Second, the assailant was powerful. Pete was not overly tall at five feet, ten inches, but he was wiry, and rock climbing would have made him very strong. Third, the murderer wanted Pete to know who he was. The assailant had attacked Pete from behind and strangled him, but not to death. He stopped at a point, pulled him down to the deck, knelt over him and stabbed him. There were signs that Pete had continued to struggle after he was down on the deck. Brie had found strands of his hair, with skin tags attached, caught in the cracks between the deck planks. They had been pulled forcibly from Pete's head during the struggle. The murderer was exacting retribution for something Pete had done, and he wanted the satisfaction of knowing that his face was the last thing Pete would ever see.

Brie finished with Rob's duffel and toiletries. Nothing there of interest except a bottle of Chivas Regal and a heavy plastic tumbler. She hadn't seen Rob drinking but assumed he liked a nightcap before turning in. No wonder Alyssa was able to leave the cabin to go up on deck and smoke; Rob was probably out for the count.

She searched Alyssa's duffel next, as well as a small make-up bag. Nothing interesting there except for a number of condoms tucked into a box containing hair waxing strips. Had Alyssa hidden them there? Brie checked around the rest of the cabin, lifting up the pad on the berth and checking the small cabinet under the wash stand. Nothing incriminating here.

She walked across the passageway and entered John's cabin. A duffel, holding his belongings, sat next to his berth. Brie searched through it thoroughly, hoping he wouldn't notice she'd been there. She found two black tee-shirts that looked like they hadn't been worn. Remembering the black fibers under Pete's nails, she checked them carefully for any sign of wear. Nothing. The cabin contained little else except John's books and charts. No clues to his personal life, which she couldn't help wondering about—especially the girlfriend part. Brie stepped out the door and back into her cabin. She put on her raincoat and headed up the ladder.

Pulling her hood up against the rain, she walked forward to the other companionway that descended to the cabins of Tim Pelletier and the Thackerays. John was standing at the foot of the galley companionway talking to the passengers and blocking the view up onto the deck. Smart boy, she thought. She was able to get down to the forward cabins without being seen.

Brie shed her raincoat in the passageway and started with Tim's cabin. She noticed he had packed light. Passengers were encouraged to bring a minimal number of things on a windjammer cruise because the cabins were tiny. Other than warm clothes at this time of year and rain gear, there just wasn't much you needed, but John had encouraged the passengers to bring a book, a camera, binoculars, and maybe a journal to write in.

Tucked among Tim's clothing Brie found a 5x7 framed photograph of a group of young people on what looked like a hike or camping trip. Tim was standing to the right with a pretty red-headed girl. They had their arms around each other's waists, and she was leaning against his shoulder. Brie wondered if this was the woman immortalized on Tim's chest. She found nothing else in his cabin. As she stepped out the door, she heard George say "Ready with the first round of pancakes."

Brie walked a few feet across the passageway and entered the Thackerays' cabin. She had little hope of finding bloody clothing in any of the cabins. It would have been too easy for the killer to throw any blood-stained item overboard, and it would have disappeared on the outgoing tide. Also, a few rocks and a plastic bag would have sent anything incriminating to the bottom. As far as any blood on one of the rain slickers, it would have run right off in the heavy rain that was falling last night. Anyway, she guessed the killer wouldn't have tried to sneak up on Pete wearing a yellow coat.

Brie searched quickly through Howard's duffel, finding nothing incriminating. She wasn't surprised—Howard wasn't much of a suspect. It was always possible, though, that he and Will had collaborated in the crime—she'd seen odder things than that in her career. But Will's belongings yielded nothing interesting either.

The cabin contained a bunk bed. Brie checked underneath the pad on the lower bunk. Nothing. Climbing up the ladder she lifted the pad on the top bunk and scanned underneath. Something black in the far back corner caught her eye. She crawled up on top of the bunk and into the back corner, where she lifted up the pad. Stuffed down between the bunk board and the wall was a black sock containing something. She pulled it out and looked inside. It held a marline spike that was approximately eight inches long. Keeping hold of the bottom of it with the sock, she rotated it slowly. There, engraved on the side, were the initials P. M .

Pete had mentioned last night that his marline spike was missing, and that he thought he might have dropped it on deck during the storm. Had he gone to get a spare from the storeroom? Or had someone else taken one of the spares after Scott mentioned them and later stabbed Pete with it? And finally, if Will found Pete's marline spike on deck, why had he kept it after Pete was murdered? Brie added these to the growing list of questions she'd begun compiling. She bunched up the top of the sock in her hand and crawled down off the bunk. Suddenly, she sensed someone was there. Whirling around, she found John standing in the doorway no more than four feet away, watching her. He saw the fear in her eyes.

"I'm sorry if I startled you, Brie," he said. "I didn't want to say anything when I saw you up there. I thought you'd jump and bang your head. Sorry."

"What are you doing down here?" Brie's tone had an edge.

"I came down to get a lamp from the storeroom. One of the ones in the galley just ran dry. The sky's so dark today we need the lamps burning down there. George is about to serve up omelets. Are you nearly finished?"

"This cabin was my last stop." She stepped past DuLac into the passageway and picked up her raincoat. She slipped the sock containing the marline spike into a large pocket on the inside and put on the coat. Still feeling uneasy about his presence, she didn't comment about what she'd found, nor did he ask.

DuLac walked into the storeroom and was out a few seconds later with another hurricane lamp. "From where everybody is seated at the table, they can't see you coming up this ladder. When I get up on deck, I'll pretend I've just run into you."

He started up the ladder with her behind him. Once they

were both up he said in a slightly raised voice, "There you are, Brie. I was just coming to get you. George is serving up the omelets right now."

"Great, I'm starved."

She followed him down to the galley, where everyone sat in utter silence. Tension and distrust hung in the air as thick and heavy as a north Atlantic fog. Brie exchanged sober greetings with the group. She took off her coat, laid it on the floor next to the bench, and slid in alongside Scott. John sat at the end of the opposite bench.

George was serving up ham and cheese omelets and passing the plates around. A large steaming platter of blueberry pancakes sat in the middle of the table waiting to be circulated. "Captain, why don't you start the pancakes, butter and syrup around," he said. John helped himself to two pancakes and sent the platter down his side of the table to Howard, Will and Tim. It was then passed across to Alyssa, Rob, Scott and Brie. George snagged two for his plate, set them back on the stove to stay warm, and sat down next to the captain.

"Can I pour you some coffee, Brie?" Scott asked, reaching for one of the carafes.

"Thanks." Brie held her mug over and immediately noticed that he was pouring with his left hand. She amused herself with the thought that she could wrap up this murder quickly, if six of the other seven people present would just pick up their forks and eat with their left hands. They could all pounce on the remaining culprit, tie him up with some heavy line and lower him into the hold for safekeeping until the Coast Guard arrived. Her fantasy evaporated like sweat on a windy day as all seven of the others picked up their forks and started eating with right-handed abandon.

Brie studied the group surreptitiously as she ate her omelet, noticing particularly the shift in both Rob's and Alyssa's demeanors. Rob's offensiveness had disappeared, revealing a well of concern for Alyssa. Alyssa, for her part, displayed a mood as gray as the baggy sweat suit she was wearing. The make-up and flirta-tiousness were gone, replaced by puffy red eyes and wan lips. She forked in her pancakes with an intensity that caused Brie to imagine them as mortar for her crumbling emotional dam. Tim clung to his corner at the opposite end of the table, as if trying to become one with the hull of the ship, and Will's eyes darted nerv-ously around the table between bites of food, like a rat with his cheese, checking for the oversized tabby cat. Then there was Howard, who just looked sad—the look of a man who was old enough to have seen as much death as he'd like to for one lifetime. John was totally unreadable, so complete was the neutrality he dis-played. And George's usually jovial aura had been replaced by a nervous tic in his left eye.

Brie got up and went over to the stove to spear another pan-cake. On the way back she paused. From where she stood, she had a good view of everyone's face as she posed her question.

"Did anyone talk to or see Pete during his watch last night?" she asked.

Everyone shook their heads or said "no." But in both George and Alyssa there was a nuance of expression absent in the others. Neither of them made eye contact with Brie. It was exactly what she'd hoped for. She suspected that each of them had seen Pete sometime between 1:00 and 3:00 A.M. It was a place to start. She sat back down, and everyone continued eating in a thick silence.

Howard finally spoke, sending a ripple of relief though the group. "The captain's told us we'll be going to the inn this morn-ing, where you'll be asking us questions," he said to Brie. "I, for one, will be glad to get off the ship and go for the walk, even if it is still raining." He tried for an upbeat tone in his voice.

"It'll feel good to stretch our legs," Brie said. "The inn is a very comfortable place, and I think we could use some comfort right now." Her comment took some of the tension from the air.

"I'll prepare a nice lunch at the inn," George said, trying to add his two cents of cheerfulness to the pot.

78

"If there's anything you need help with on the ship, Captain, what with Pete gone and all, I'll be glad to be of service," said Rob.

Everyone stared at him like he'd just grown another head.

"I appreciate that, Rob," DuLac said diplomatically and then turned to the others. "As soon as everyone's done we'll get the dishes cleaned up and start for the island. You should all bring along whatever will add to your comfort during the day. I have some books in my cabin—mostly sea literature of one kind and another—you're all welcome to take a look and borrow anything you like. And Glenn and Betty have a great library up at the inn."

Brie stood up and retrieved a piece of paper and a pen from her raincoat. "Before you leave I need each of you to write down your full name followed by your date of birth." She half expected Will to gve her a hard time about it, and when she glanced at him, he had opened his mouth as if he were about to speak. Catching the don't-mess-with-me look in her eyes, he closed it again and said nothing. No one else asked any questions, and each of them stopped to sign the sheet as they got up from the table.

George had set a large pan of hot soapy water off the stove onto the end of the table, so everyone could wash their dishes. A smaller rubber pan held clean water for rinsing. Each person took his turn at the dishpan, then dried his plate, cup and utensils and handed them to George, who stowed them in a cabinet at the back of the galley. One by one, they disappeared up the ladder to collect anything they wanted to bring with them for the day.

Brie took DuLac aside. "Captain, can you call the crew together for a brief meeting up on the stern of the ship? It will give me a chance to search their quarters."

"How much time do you need?" he asked.

"Ten minutes should do it."

"No problem. As a matter of fact, I have a few things I need to go over with them before we leave the ship. The crew's sleeping area is accessed from behind the companionway ladder in the galley. You saw Scott go in there last night for his guitar."

"Thanks, I'll see you on deck in a few minutes, then."

Within fifteen minutes the passengers and crew were climbing down to the yawl boat wearing their rain gear. John released the line holding the boat to the stern of the *Maine Wind*. As Scott steered toward the docks of Lobsterman's Cove, Brie wondered about the edginess she'd seen in George and the watchfulness that Will had displayed. Could their reactions be written off as fear of a killer in their midst, or was something much more sinister behind the change?

8

THE YELLOW-CLAD ENTOURAGE wound up the hill toward the inn like some mustard-worshipping cult on the way to its temple. As they trudged along the wet road, Brie, who was bringing up the rear of the parade with John, mentally reviewed the list of suspects, motives and questions that were accumulating in her mind. The most obvious motive belonged to Rob. If he caught Alyssa with Pete, he may have murdered him in a jealous rage. From Alyssa's reaction to her question at breakfast, Brie guessed she had seen Pete at some point before he died.

Will had the other obvious motive. He killed Pete because Pete got the job he wanted. Hard to believe, Brie thought, but she'd seen stranger things. That marline spike she'd found in Will's bunk troubled her, though. Had he put it there? Why would he keep it if he had murdered Pete? Maybe he had the kind of devious mind that thought in layers. You're guilty, so do the thing a guilty person would never do, and it makes you look innocent. Kind of a reverse psychology strategy. And in the same vein—the Will's-a-devious-thinker vein—if you're going to commit a murder, why not bring your dear old dad along to remove some more suspicion from yourself?

As they climbed up the hill, mud stuck to their shoes, making obscene little noises. So much for the obvious motives, Brie thought. Now, moving on to the weak motive department. That would be John's department—the captain-kills-second-mate-for-disobedience department. Suppose Pete, despite the captain's warning, met Alyssa during his watch—in fact went beyond merely meeting her. The captain wouldn't need to kill him when he could simply fire him. Either way, he'd be out a second mate. Furthermore, she'd found nothing when she searched John's cabin except the broken radio transmitter, and others had had the opportunity to tamper with that. If Brie was any judge of character—and she was—John didn't have a killer's bone in his body. And anyway, despite Pete's shortcomings, John liked him. That was obvious from her interview with him this morning. So, pending some profound hidden motive that might rear its head, Brie felt safe eliminating the captain from her list of suspects. She heaved a sigh of relief as they trudged along.

"You okay, Brie?" John had been walking beside her in silence.

"Yup. Just processing," she said. "It's a big part of the job. Never become a detective if you don't like to think. It's nine parts analysis and one part action." She returned to her thoughts as they climbed toward the inn. Howard was too old to have committed the murder. His age and short stature ruled him out, along with the heart medication she'd found in his duffel. Sixty-eight-year-old men with heart conditions don't overpower strong twenty-eight-year-old men.

Alyssa was unwise in her choices, but she didn't seem malicious. It was obvious to Brie, from Alyssa's apparent state of emotional collapse, that she somehow felt responsible for Pete's death. But she did not think for a minute that Alyssa was actually the killer. She remembered Alyssa boarding the ship on Friday evening, carrying her duffel with two hands and not having an easy time with it. Brie had lifted that duffel this morning and could have easily carried it in one hand. Alyssa didn't have the strength to kill Pete, unless, of course, she had an accomplice. Brie hoped questioning her would reveal why she was acting guilty.

No, she thought, the front-runners were definitely Rob, Will, Tim, and George. There was something hidden in Tim's life. Something he brooded about but didn't discuss. Whether it related in any way to Pete or the murder, she would have to find out. And George's behavior was also odd. Either he knew something about the murder or he had some motive for killing Pete.

As she mulled over the suspects, the inn came into view above the last curve in the road. Anyone lulled into a Zen-like state by their climb in the rain was slapped back to consciousness as they crossed the wide lawn against a stinging northeast wind. All nine of them broke into a jog, heading for the shelter of the porch. John unlocked the heavy front door and they stepped inside the inn.

The smell of lilacs from the pitcher on the hall table engulfed them. They removed their raincoats and hung them on a large brass coat rack that stood next to a parson's bench in the front corner of the hall.

"I'm going to set up shop in the library, Captain," Brie said. "When I'm ready, I'll come and get you, one by one, for questioning." Brie padded across the polished wood floor in her socks and disappeared through the second door back on the right.

"I'll give everyone a tour of the downstairs and then you can settle in wherever you're comfortable." John led the group through the door on the left into the living room. Glenn had left a fire burning in the fireplace, and John added a couple of logs to the glowing embers. He ushered everyone through the dining room and into the kitchen. Betty had left an urn of hot coffee next to a tray of mugs. Alongside the tray sat a large pan of blueberry cobbler with a note that everyone should enjoy it throughout the day.

John smiled. Betty was the perfect innkeeper. She mothered every-body, and because of that the inn had thrived, supported by a loyal clientele who wouldn't miss their annual visit to Snug Harbor Bed and Breakfast for anything. But he knew there was another side to Betty. She was a survivor. Her life had called for a kind of strength most people would never have to find—the strength that allows a mother to go on after the death of her only child.

A few of the passengers helped themselves to coffee, and John led them from the kitchen back out into the hall, where he pointed out a bathroom tucked under the staircase. He indicated the library door, which Brie had closed, and then led everyone up the hall and into the game room directly across from the living room. A massive billiard table with ornately carved legs sat at the far end, and comfortable furniture in muted greens, golds and rusts filled the rest of the room. Two sofas, chairs and tables were grouped around a large entertainment center. In front of the windows, two wooden game tables, each with a set of upholstered chairs, invited guests to play a game of cards or Scrabble and take in the ocean panorama that stretched out before them.

In the library Brie prepared for a long day of questioning the passengers and crew. At least this was a great room to be stuck in. Being surrounded by books was one of the most comforting things she could imagine. Since childhood, she'd always loved curling up in a big chair with a good book. She looked around the room. Except for a large French window at one end, the fireplace and the door, every inch of wall space was covered with handsome walnut bookcases. A large mahogany desk sat in front of the window, facing into the room, and soft leather furniture and pol-ished wood tables invited guests to settle in. An oriental rug of bold reds and blues warmed the already inviting room.

Brie stepped over to the fireplace. Glenn had set a fire there, and she stoked it back to life. Checking her watch, she walked over to the desk—10:40—time to get started. She unbuckled a large fanny pack from around her waist, zipped it open and took out an assortment of items she had brought with her. The small tape recorder, a note pad with the names and addresses of the passengers and crew, the sheet containing the birth dates, a pocket phone directory, and finally, a length of half-inch braided rope, grayed from lots of handling. She also took out the sock containing the marline spike that she had found in Will's bunk, opened the top drawer of the desk and put it inside. Then she sat down in the leather swivel chair behind the desk, flipped open her phone directory and dialed up Garrett Parker at the Minneapolis Police Department.

A voice came across the crackly connection. "Parker here."

"Gare! Hi, it's Brie."

"Brie! My God, what a surprise! I thought you'd gone completely underground. Where are you? There's a lot of static on this line."

"Well, I'm on an island off the coast of Maine."

"Jeezus, when you run away you're serious about it, aren't you."

"You know me—never do anything halfway."

"So, why do I feel like you're not calling because you miss my voice?"

"I need your help, Gare."

"I can hop a plane this afternoon, kiddo."

"Thanks, but it's not that kind of help. There's been a murder."

Silence spun down the wire.

"Well, well, Brie. You can run but you can't hide."

"Very funny, Gare. Listen, I'd like to give you a list of names and birthdates to run through NCIC."

"No problem. Anything else?"

"Could you do a little digging—check the police departments in their towns of residence and see if you come up with anything?"

"It'll cost you! Should we say dinner and drinks?"

Brie chuckled. "Well, okay. It's a deal."

"So, when *are* you coming home, Brie? There just isn't anyone else around here that can make a decent cup of coffee. We need you."

"That sexist humor won't help your cause, Gare. Anyway, I'm not ready to come home yet."

"It's been six weeks, Brie."

"I took a leave, remember? Anyway, do you know how much vacation you pile up when you haven't taken any time off in eight years? I could stay gone for six months and still be drawing pay."

"Well, I wish you'd think about it. There *are* people around here who really miss you."

"Thanks, Gare, that's nice." Brie was surprised by this conversation. Garrett was a colleague in the department, but she'd never thought of him as anything more than that. Had she missed something? Because her antenna was picking up more than professional interest here.

"So, give me the names and I'll get started, Brie. And I need a number where I can reach you."

Brie read off the list of names, addresses and birth dates, gave Garrett the phone number to the inn, thanked him for his help and hung up. She opened the top drawer of the desk, found some blank paper and started jotting down questions that she intended to ask Scott and George. Then she got up and headed out into the hall to locate Scott. She found him in the TV room playing a game of billiards with Tim.

"Hate to break up your game, Scott, but I'd like to start with you," she said. Scott set down his cue and followed her into the library. "Why don't you pull a chair over to the other side of the desk."

Scott picked up a high-backed chair and placed it in front of the desk. "Boy, you could get lost in here," he remarked. "This would be a dangerous room to have in my house. I'd never get anything done."

Brie checked and started the recorder. Scott stared at it briefly and then sat back in the chair.

Brie began. "What do you do in the off season, Scott, when you're not crewing on the *Maine Wind*?

"I work as an independent tutor during the school year and also give music lessons. Five years ago Captain DuLac encouraged me to go back to school. I took a double major in math and music at the University of Maine. I just finished a year ago. It's fulfilling work, teaching kids—I like it a lot. My kids fall into two distinct groups. The math kids are usually struggling, and the music kids are striving, so I deal with a whole range of attitudes and abilities. It keeps me humble, I'll tell you that much."

"Did you know Pete before he came to work on the *Maine Wind*?"

"No. We met in May after the captain hired him. I'd seen him around Camden and Rockport—he crewed on another windjammer last year—but I'd never met him."

"When was the last time you saw Pete alive?"

"When he came on deck last night to relieve me after the first watch."

Brie jotted down a few notes before continuing.

"After he took over the watch at 1:00 A.M., did you hear anything unusual?"

"I was dead tired from the day we put in out there. I was asleep before my head hit the pillow. A while later, though, I was awakened by voices. Pete and George were having what sounded like a heated discussion."

"Could you hear what they were saying?"

"No. But I knew it was them—they were out in the galley. They weren't exactly yelling but their voices had an edge to them."

"Do you know what time that was?"

"I checked my watch. It was 1:45."

"Were you awake when George came back to bed?"

"I was just starting to drift back off."

"Did you ask him what the problem was?"

"I didn't think it was any of my business. You know how it is—when you live on a ship nobody has a lot of space. You don't ask questions that could create tension. Any problems with another crew member have to go to the captain."

Brie rocked back in the leather chair. Scott was totally matter-of-fact in his responses. No hesitation here, and, it would seem, nothing to hide.

"You sleep in the same area as George. Have you ever known him to get up at night?"

"Sometimes he'll forget to do something out in the galley that's essential to breakfast. I've occasionally heard him get up in the night."

"How did he and Pete seem to get along?"

"Okay, I guess. Although I've overheard Pete say a couple of things to George that seemed more like bullying than teasing. George doesn't have that much contact with Pete, though. He's below deck a lot, and Pete and I are topside helping the captain. Personally, I thought Pete was a little immature for his age, but I found him easy enough to get along with, and he was a good sailor."

Brie had actually thought the same thing, finding Scott to be the more mature even though he was the younger of the two mates.

"Could George have gotten up again last night without your knowledge?"

"Normally I'd say no, because our berths are so close together down there. But I suppose it's possible if I was really sound asleep."

"Looking back, is there anything else that seems unusual or in any way significant which could relate to the murder?"

Scott hesitated.

"What?"

"It's more something I sensed," he said, uncomfortably. "I can't say why, but it felt like there was an uneasiness between Pete and Tim the first day or two of this cruise. It could be they're just very different from one another. Pete's outgoing, and Tim's quite withdrawn."

Brie had noticed Scott's tendency to refer to Pete as if he were still alive. Not unusual in these situations, she thought. It reflects some level of denial in the mind following a sudden traumatic occurrence.

"Well, that's all for now, Scott."

"But don't leave town, right?"

Brie laughed. "Actually, I'd like to see you pull that off. Could you send George in next? And don't reveal our conversation, okay?"

"Okay." Scott got up and left the library.

George drifted into the room on a current of uncertainty. This is not the jovial man of a couple days ago, Brie thought.

"Come sit down, George. Make yourself comfortable."

George crossed to the desk, sat down on the edge of the chair, and looked at her with misgiving.

"This is hard for all of us, George. I just have a few questions for you."

"I'm ready," he replied, with all the enthusiasm of the patient about to receive a shot.

"When did you last see Pete alive?"

"Actually, I ran into him in the galley last night during his watch. I know I indicated otherwise at breakfast—probably because I was nervous about seeing him so close to the time of his death."

"Did the two of you talk?"

"Briefly, but it was more of an argument." Brie noticed that the tic in the corner of George's left eye had reactivated.

"Tell me what happened."

"I woke up when Scott came in from his watch. I was having a hard time going back to sleep. I remembered I was low on wood for the stove for morning, so I thought I'd go up on deck and bring some forward from the hold. I went out to the galley and was restacking the wood next to the stove when Pete came down and asked what I was doing." George paused a moment, conjuring the scene. "I told him I couldn't sleep and I was going to get some wood from the hold for morning. He said to forget it because the noise would disturb the captain. That made me angry—after all, I've been on the *Maine Wind* for five years. I said he couldn't tell me what to do, and that I certainly knew how to get wood out of the hold without waking up the whole ship." George sat back in the chair, seeming to relax a bit now that he was telling his story. "Pete was standing in front of the ladder blocking the way up, so I told him to move. I couldn't believe he was acting like that. It almost felt like there was some other reason he didn't want me up there."

This made Brie think about Alyssa's expression at breakfast when she'd asked if anyone had seen Pete alive during his watch. Maybe Alyssa and Pete had a rendezvous planned, and George was in the way. Or maybe Alyssa was already up on deck and Pete didn't want George to see her.

"What did you do next, George?"

George leaned forward, gathering confidence around his words. "There was nothing I could do without getting into a shoving match with him. And that *would* have awakened people. It was one of those times where someone had to back down—I decided it would be me."

"I'd say that was the mature choice, George."

"Thanks. It made me plenty mad, though, I can tell you. But not mad enough to kill him, if that's what you're thinking."

"I'm not thinking anything yet," Brie said, tapping her pencil. "Just collecting information. Unfortunately, though, it's my job to figure out who *was* mad enough to kill him."

Brie picked up the length of rope she'd placed on the desk earlier and lazily began tying a series of figure eight knots in it as she studied George. Keeping her hands busy had a calming effect on her. Years ago she'd taken to carrying this length of rope with her during investigations. Over time it had taken on a kind of symbolism. Her lucky rope that helped her tie up loose ends and unravel the truth. She had, as an added bonus, become a master of knots—essential knowledge for any sailor.

"To be truthful, George, Scott has already mentioned that he heard you arguing with Pete last night, so I'm glad you were forthcoming about it. Is there anything else you'd like to add?"

"Not that I can think of."

"Do you know why anyone else on board may have wanted to harm Pete?"

"Well, it's no secret, after dinner last night, that Rob's got a temper. He's jealous of anyone Alyssa even looks at. Doesn't seem like enough reason to kill somebody though."

Ha, Brie thought to herself. If he only knew how often petty arguments and grudges escalated into murder. It was one of the dark facts about mankind that Brie preferred not to discuss—why give it more power than it already had? Leave George comfortable in his culinary world. She set down her rope. "Okay, George, that's all for now." She watched him get up and leave the library.

9

BRIE STOOD UP AND STRETCHED HER ARMS over her head, releasing some of the tension in her shoulders. She walked out of the library and across the hall to the kitchen. George was there going through the cabinets, starting to plan lunch. She poured herself a mug of coffee and headed for the game room. Alyssa, Rob, Will and Howard were watching the video of *Raiders of the Lost Ark*. John and Scott were playing pool, and Tim was sitting at the game table near the front windows working on a jigsaw puzzle.

"Alyssa, I'd like to talk to you next," Brie said. Alyssa was curled up on the sofa next to Rob under a faded quilt. Leaning over and kissing his cheek, she stood up and followed Brie into the library.

Brie moved over to the fireplace and set a couple of logs onto the grate. She watched as small tongues of flame shot up from the thick bed of embers to lick the sides of the wood. A particularly strong gust of wind pinged rain against the window behind the desk, drawing her gaze from the fire. Water sheeted the outer glass, moving like translucent mercury.

"Come sit down, Alyssa." Brie motioned her toward the interrogation seat. After Alyssa had settled in, Brie said, "It must have been terrible finding Pete like that."

"I'll never get that image out of my mind." Alyssa rolled the bottom edge of her sweatshirt up and down as she gazed out the window.

"What made you go up on deck at that hour of the night?"

"I couldn't sleep—I wanted to have a cigarette."

"It wasn't the first time you were up on deck during Pete's watch last night, was it?"

Alyssa lowered her head. Tears of fear and regret flowed down her face and dropped onto the front of her misshapen sweatshirt. "I've been playing this game of manipulation with Rob so long I can't even remember when it started. Before we were married I think, and now it's led to..."

"Led to what, Alyssa? Did Rob find you up on deck with Pete?"

"No." She was sobbing now. "But I think he knew."

"Knew what, Alyssa? Did you have sex with Pete?" Alyssa's silence gave Brie her answer. Rain swept across the window. "How could you do that when Rob is like a bottle of nitro on the edge of a high shelf?"

"I don't know," she sobbed. "The worst part is I think Rob really loves me. But my behavior makes him angry, and his ignoring what I want and need pushes me further away. So now we just get each other's attention by acting outrageous. I provoke his jealousy, and he wraps it around me like a straitjacket, suffocating me. I can see we've both been wrong, but I don't know how to start over. I feel like I'm locked out of my house in the cold, and I've lost my key."

Brie leaned back in her chair and studied Alyssa. "Honesty is the key, Alyssa," she finally said. "In fact, it's a kind of skeleton key—you'd be amazed what it will open."

Alyssa looked up, uncertain.

"It looks like you've taken the first step by being honest with yourself."

"I just hope I'm not too late." Alyssa's despondent gaze found the window.

"What time were you up on deck with Pete?" Brie asked, bringing Alyssa's focus back to the interview.

"I went up there at about 1:45."

"Weren't you worried that Rob would wake up and find you missing?"

"Rob always has a couple of drinks before bed—nothing wakes him up after that."

Alyssa had managed to convince herself of that, but Brie wasn't so sure.

"So, you went on deck at 1:45. What happened after that?"

"I was just walking toward the bow when I heard Pete arguing with George, so I stayed back where he wouldn't see me."

"Do you know what they were arguing about?"

"No, not exactly. I just heard Pete accusing George of being gay."

Brie's head jerked up from the notes she'd been writing.

"Go on," she said.

"He was saying something about how he wouldn't crew on a ship with someone who was gay. Pete just had this irrational hatred of gays, and he told me he'd heard a rumor about George."

"And what time did you leave Pete and go back to your cabin?"

"It was about 2:20 when I headed back down below deck. I went to use the head and was in there about five minutes before going back to our cabin."

"Did you hear anything unusual at all after you went back to bed?"

"I fell asleep pretty quick. I was tired."

"Do you know if Rob left the cabin after you came back in?"

"No! I mean, I'm sure he didn't." Alyssa sat forward nervously, and Brie guessed from her response that Rob had indeed left the cabin. The downside of interrogation was that almost everybody lied about something. Brie had learned long ago that finding the truth was somewhat like sifting through sand looking for salt.

She pressed her a little more. "You say you were so tired you fell asleep immediately. Isn't it possible you wouldn't have awakened if Rob got up?"

"No," she said emphatically. "That's not possible."

"So, if you were sleeping soundly with Rob, what caused you to wake up and need a cigarette a mere 45 minutes later?"

Alyssa squirmed. "There was a lot of lightning. I think that's what woke me. I put on my raincoat and went up on deck for a smoke. I'm trying to quit—just one more weakness in my character, I guess."

And lying rounds it out nicely, Brie thought, wondering if she should repeat the honesty speech. At least Alyssa was transparent in her lying which meant, maybe, there was hope for reform. What was more, this last lie had a more noble purpose—it was obviously meant to protect Rob.

"Well, that's all I need from you right now, Alyssa. Why don't you give me about ten minutes and then send Rob in. And please don't discuss our conversation." Alyssa got up and walked to the door. She paused with her hand on the knob as if debating about something. Then she opened the door and stepped out, closing it softly behind her.

Brie swiveled the big chair around, propped her feet up on the window sill, and thought about egg noodles. The thought brought immediate comfort. Stress, confusion and anxiety almost always led to a healthy serving of egg noodles with plenty of butter, usually followed by a long walk. Her private formula for getting her head straight, it harked back to her childhood and her mother's homemade spaetzle.

Old Mrs. Hoffmeister, their next door neighbor on Cherry Street, had passed on the wonders of spaetzle-making to Edna Beaumont, who didn't have a German bone in her body. For some mysterious reason, known only to Edna, spaetzle was never made except at the lake. It was a time-consuming process that ironically flourished in the primitive setting of their rustic lake cabin, as if the making of spaetzle somehow lent itself to a lack of electricity and running water.

Brie remembered how her mom would sit on the front porch of the cabin with the big stoneware bowl in her lap working the thick dough for the spaetzle. Then she'd fire up the old Coleman stove out on the picnic table and put on a big pot of water. Brie and her brothers would roll small pieces of the dough with their hands. They'd drop them into the boiling water and wait impatiently 'til they rose to the top. Edna would scoop up steaming bowls of the wonderful stuff and add dollops of butter. The three siblings would plop down on top of the picnic table—feet on the bench, lake out in front—to enjoy the spoils of their labor.

Brie stared out the window at the storm, but the rain fell in her heart. She felt a sudden longing for things that could never be reclaimed—childhood and the comfort of family. Mom had loved that cabin—loved it! But Dad had loved the open water. He was a Mainer. The sea and sailing were in his blood. He had finally cajoled mom into selling the cabin so he could have his boat on Lake Superior. Brie and her brothers had loved boat and cabin alike, just as they had loved both parents. And mom—she'd gone along with it the way women often did. But she was never comfortable on the boat. What was more, she had never again made spaetzle, even though Brie had repeatedly begged her.

Edna *had* made a stand when she and Tom Beaumont were first married. She had badly wanted to stay in Minnesota, and he had finally agreed. In the beginning there are other things men want badly, and it makes them willing to compromise. But for

Edna, staying in Minnesota had been like taking out a long-term mortgage she would pay back in a million ways over the years, as if that decision were always accruing interest. Giving up the lake cabin for his boat was just one of the ways Mom had stayed current on the debt. And then the heart attack, just four years after the boat. All was lost—all. Dad had no life insurance, and Mom had sold the boat and everything else just to keep the family going.

There was a knock on the door and George popped his head in. "Anything I can get for you, Brie?"

"Egg noodles?"

"Ah, I'm not sure..."

"Just kidding, George." She turned her chair around. "Whatever you're planning for lunch will be fine."

"How about a tuna melt and a bowl of corn chowder?"

"Sounds great. Could you bring it in here? I'd like to make some notes while I eat."

"No problem." He was about to close the door when Rob hove into view and asked if he should come in.

"How long 'til lunch, George?" Brie asked.

"About fifteen minutes."

"That'll give us time. Come in, Rob, and have a seat."

Rob advanced toward the chair with a physical presence which alone would have placed him high on the list of suspects. Sitting down, he leveled his gaze at Brie and spoke in a surprisingly controlled tone. "I didn't kill Pete. I just want to say that right up front. I know I'm probably your most likely suspect after the way I acted last night." He seemed to have relinquished his bravado and antagonism, which, no doubt, had served as a suitable shield for a male ego badly battered by Alyssa's antics.

"Why don't you tell me when you last saw Pete?" Brie said.

"I went up on deck at 2:55 A.M. I know because I checked my watch just before leaving the cabin. I was going to have it out with him—I knew Alyssa had been with him. She thinks I'm asleep when she comes in like that. I never am. Anyway, I waited for her to fall asleep, and then I went up there to find him. Well, I found him all right—I found him dead. I panicked since I had a pretty good motive for killing him myself, especially considering I was planning on beating the shit out of him. I should have called the captain, but I assumed either he or Scott would come on deck at the change of the watch and find Pete."

"Has it occurred to you that Alyssa could have killed him?"

"Come on! That's just not possible. She's not strong enough. And what would her motive be?"

"Maybe Pete threatened to tell you about their affair."

"I can't believe even he would be that stupid. Unless he had a death wish."

"Apparently he didn't need one."

"I just should have gone for the captain when I discovered his body," Rob said again. "I'll never forgive myself for that. It was horrible for Alyssa to find him. I never meant to fall back to sleep, but she woke up when I came back in and could see I was upset. She asked what was wrong, and I told her I was feeling restless. She told me to get back in bed and she'd rub my back—she knows that relaxes me. I can't believe I fell asleep."

Brie guessed the truth was that when Rob came back in upset, Alyssa was worried enough to go back up on deck. Maybe that's why she thought it might be too late to salvage their relationship. She must believe that Rob had killed Pete. In Brie's mind it was also still the strongest possibility.

"There was something else, too," Rob said.

"Go ahead."

"I could swear I saw something move up toward the front of the ship as I started back down the ladder to our cabin. It may have been just a shadow, but I don't think so. I was a Marine—we were trained to spot subtle movement. I'm ninety percent certain someone was up there. I headed back toward the bow to look around, but found nothing."

"Could you see well enough to tell if someone went down one of the front companionways?"

"They could have ducked down into the forward cabins, but I had a view of the galley companionway as I walked forward. A kerosene lamp was burning down there, so I think I would have seen anyone heading down that ladder. I went down into the forward compartment and checked the storeroom and the head. Nothing. I tried the doors to the cabins, but they were locked. There was nothing else to be done, so I went back to my cabin."

Brie studied Rob for a moment, hoping to get a gut sense of whether he was being truthful, but she wasn't picking up a vibe one way or the other. If he *was* telling the truth, she now had a lock on the time of death. The killer struck during the 35 minutes between Alyssa's leaving Pete at 2:20 and Rob's going on deck at 2:55. Tim, Will and Howard had those forward cabins, and conceivably George could have ducked into one of their cabins if the door was unlocked. Scott had no apparent motive, in addition to being left-handed, and Brie felt certain that the killer was right-handed. She jotted down a few notes.

"Is there anything else?" Rob asked with some urgency. "I'd like to get back to Alyssa."

Brie looked up from her notepad. "That's all for now." She watched him move toward the door, but as he turned the knob to leave she stopped him. "You know Rob, amazingly, sometimes something good can come out of a crisis like this. Assuming you're telling the truth, that is."

He turned slowly back around. "I'm sorry I was rude to you last night, Brie. It was uncalled for. You're okay." With that he strode out of the library.

Brie walked over to the fireplace and set three logs onto the grate. She stepped back and watched them ignite. Holding her hands out to the warmth, her gaze came unfocused as she stared deep into the flames. Wind and rain rattled at the window and somewhere in the storm a gull cried. An errant spark snapped out of the fire and struck her outstretched hand as if to say, don't get too close. Brie stepped back, rubbing her hand, and wished she were far away.

10

BRIE'S MOOD WAS BEING SUCKED TOWARD a black hole when a knock on the door reeled her back. John stuck his head in. "George says you're eating lunch in here. Would you like some company?"

"Sure!" She took so much comfort in his face at that moment that it startled her. "And, if you don't mind detective-talk while you eat, maybe I can bounce a few thoughts off you."

"Hang on. I'll go see if George can put some starch in my shirt."

Brie laughed. "That should be an interesting look on flannel." She reveled for a moment in John's humor and smile, relaxing into them as she would a warm sweater. Something about him had a resuscitating effect on her. He was the salt air straight off the Atlantic, and she liked the feel of him on her tattered psyche. Oddly enough he felt like home—like Mom and Dad—like nights around the Monopoly board, and breezy vacations on blue Minnesota lakes.

George appeared in the doorway carrying a large wooden tray. A savory aroma ushered him into the room, and he set the lunch down on a circular table between two chairs. On the tray were two miniature cast-iron kettles filled with thick, creamy corn chowder, and two rose-colored plates with toasted tuna melts, served open face on thick slices of homemade bread. There were also two compotes of fresh fruit, two bowls of Betty's blueberry cobbler and a carafe of coffee. "Enjoy, folks," George said as he headed for the door.

"Thanks, George," Brie called after him.

"So, should we sit by the window or the fire?" John asked.

"Now, that's a difficult choice. I've seen an awful lot of rain in the past two days, and the fire just attacked me."

"Let's try the fire. I'll make sure you're safe," John said, giving her a look that could have liquefied granite.

"Okay." It came out as a strangled squeak. Boy, Brie thought, Detective Beaumont, victimized by her hormones, becomes a tongue-tied idiot. She took it as a sign that she might be losing control here. Lately, her feelings had been about as controllable as a roller coaster going over the big drop.

"Do you think it's safe for both of us to be in here?" Brie asked.

"I'm not sure I want it to be safe." John smiled a devilish smile.

"What I mean is..."

"I know what you mean, Brie. There's a murderer in our midst, but hopefully he's taking a lunch break right now."

"This is no joke, you know," Brie said, a hint of irritation now.

"You're right. I don't know why I said that." John held his hands in a stick-um-up position. "Everyone's in the kitchen eating, and I told Scott to keep an eye on things. I won't be in here long. Okay?"

"I guess so," Brie said hesitantly.

John pulled a low coffee table over in front of the fireplace.

Then he grabbed two of the seat cushions from the sofa and placed them on either side of the table. Brie unclipped her gun and put it in the desk. She carried the tray over and distributed the contents into two place settings, and she and John sat down, cross-legged, in front of the fire to enjoy the lunch.

"So, I guess I'm not at the top of your suspect list since you just took off your gun."

Brie raised an eyebrow, but instead of responding, tried her corn chowder.

"Are you good with it—the gun, I mean?"

Brie wondered why men were so enthralled with guns. "I used to think so," she said. "But when it mattered most…" Her voice trailed off.

"Sorry, Brie." John lowered his head, appalled at his lack of forethought.

Guns were an unavoidable part of her profession, but they held no fascination for Brie. She changed the subject.

"Do you know anything about the history of the inn?" Brie asked, spooning her soup.

"A little bit. It was originally the home of a wealthy sea captain, Josiah Campbell, who retired to the island with his wife, Hannah, in the late 1880's. He wanted to create the loveliest place possible for her to make up for all the years he'd been away at sea. He hired the best craftsmen and spared no expense importing exotic materials and furnishings. Unfortunately, Hannah died only two years after their home was finished." John picked up his spoon and sampled the chowder. "After her death Josiah became quite a recluse. He had his library and his view of the sea, and that's all that seemed to matter to him. When he died the place was purchased as a private summer home by a wealthy family from New York, and ultimately by several other families. About ten years ago Glenn and Betty bought it and turned it into a bed and breakfast."

"A place like this could really grow on you," Brie said, biting into her tuna melt. George, in usual fashion, had served up a large dose of comfort cleverly disguised as lunch.

"So how's the questioning going?"

"As usual, it's raising as many questions as it's answering. What do you know about George's private life?"

"Well, not that much, I guess. George usually goes back to New York during the off season, which is six months of the year. Why do you ask?"

"Apparently Alyssa overheard him arguing with Pete last night during his watch. She said Pete accused George of being gay."

"What! I don't believe that. When George moved up here the first summer, he brought his girlfriend with him—nothing very gay about that. And that doesn't sound like Pete, either. I don't pry into the lives of my crew, but none of that seems to ring true."

Brie shrugged. "Either way, it could give George a motive. Scott also heard him arguing with Pete at about 1:45. On another front, Rob came on deck at 2:55 in the morning and found Pete dead." She put her sandwich down.

"He didn't call anyone? You're joking."

"Said he was afraid of looking guilty. Apparently he knew Alyssa had been up on deck with Pete, and he'd had gone up there planning to, quote, 'beat the shit out of him.' "

"Was I the only one actually sleeping last night?" John asked, playing with his soup.

"I know. It's pretty amazing. And I haven't interviewed Will, Howard or Tim yet. Who knows what kind of nocturnal activities they had going on. I hope I'm not spoiling your lunch," she said, looking at his still half-full plate.

"You're not. I'm fine."

"It's also possible that Rob got a glimpse of the killer, if I can believe what he says."

"Oh?" John paused with his spoon halfway to his mouth.

"He said he saw someone in the shadows up near the bow,

just as he was heading back below decks. He went forward to check it out but found no one."

"Do you believe him?" John asked.

"I don't know. I'm slightly inclined to, but only slightly."

"So, where does that leave us?"

"I think I'll have a better feel for things after I've interviewed Tim and Will. Rob said that whoever he saw could have ducked down the forward companionway. Will and Tim both have their cabins down there."

"Did he go down and look around?" John asked, finishing his tuna melt.

"He says he checked the storeroom and also tried the cabin doors, but found nothing."

"That took some guts. Maybe he's not totally about bravado."

"Maybe not. He said he was a Marine. I have a call in to a friend of mine at the department. He's running the names I gave him to see what he comes up with." Brie polished off the rest of her tuna melt. She felt comforted by the warm food.

"So, what can I do?" John asked.

"You're doing it—just keep an eye on everyone while I'm in here doing the questioning."

"So far they've just been hanging out in the game room and taking turns getting showers. Howard, Scott and George have been down for showers, and the others are planning to go after lunch. You make sure you take some time for yourself today, Brie. Enjoy a hot shower, and stop in the game room so I can beat you at a round of pool."

Brie smiled. "We'll see who beats whom. I'm planning to grab a shower right after lunch and then finish the rest of the questioning." She poured coffee into the two mugs George had provided and offered John one of the bowls of cobbler that had been sitting off to the side. "You up for this?"

"I try to lose ten pounds every spring before the sailing season begins," John said. "The way George cooks, I know I'll gain at least that much by fall."

"I have a feeling that, with him around, I wouldn't need egg noodles."

"Come again?"

"Nothing. Just one of my comfort tactics."

"I wouldn't mind being one of your comfort tactics," he said softly.

Brie felt heat in her belly, and it wasn't from the soup. "Boy, it's getting warm by this fire; I think I'll stretch my legs." She spun around on the cushion, stood up and walked over toward the window. She heard John pad up behind her.

"I meant what I said about the comfort thing, you know. It wouldn't be imposing at all." He wrapped his hands gently around her shoulders and rested his chin on top of her head.

Brie leaned back into him—a tired traveler resting against a sturdy oak. John slipped his arms around her waist and drew her closer, nuzzling his nose against the hair just above her ear. Brie's wave of desire was just reaching tsunami proportions when a bolt of lightning, accompanied by earsplitting thunder, made them both jump. The lights flickered and went out.

"I've been waiting for the power to go out, but why now?"

John's exasperated tone would have made Brie smile, but she was busy trying to get control of her own emotions. She remembered the spark leaping out of the fireplace. Best not to get too close, she thought. She stepped away from John and walked to the desk to retrieve her gun.

"I have to go start the generator, Brie."

"You go. I'll bring the dishes out and let everyone know what's going on."

John headed through the kitchen and out the back door of the inn, telling everyone he was going to start the generator. Brie gathered up the dishes and carried the big tray back out to the kitchen. The passengers and crew were seated around the wooden tables finishing their lunches or sipping coffee.

"I'm surprised the electricity didn't go out before this, the way the wind's been blowing the last twenty-four hours," Scott said. They heard the generator roar to life and the lights came back on.

George walked over to where Brie stood looking out the back window toward a sloping wooded hill rising up behind the inn.

"As soon as the captain comes back in I'm going to grab a quick shower," she said. "Then I need to ask you a couple more questions, George."

"Sure, I'll be out here cleaning up for a while, so just call me when you're ready."

The lack of nervousness in his voice registered with Brie— obviously he wasn't too concerned about her calling him in a second time. A good sign.

"Do you know how to get down to the showers, George?"

"That door right over there." He pointed to the wall behind the tables. "Everything you need is down there—shampoo, towels, hair dryers."

Just then the captain stepped back into the kitchen. "I'm heading down for a quick shower," she said to him. "I'll be back up in a half hour or so."

"Take your time, Brie. I'll keep an eye on things here."

The shower facilities downstairs were spartan compared to the rest of the inn. But the tile floor was spotless, and there was plenty of light, thanks to several overhead fixtures. A large electric heater pumped out warmth and with the moisture from the pre-vious showers, it felt like the tropics. Brie drew a deep breath of the warm humid air. As she took a pair of soft white towels from the cabinet next to the sinks, she could feel her shoulders already beginning to relax.

She stepped into one of the small dressing cubicles that ad-joined each shower, removed her gun and folded it in one of the towels. She placed it on the end of the bench just beyond the shower curtain where she could reach it quickly if need be. She hoped she wouldn't have to respond to any emergencies in her bath towel. As she stepped naked into the shower, a brief fantasy unfolded involving John and the towel. She put her head directly under the spray to dissolve the thought.

11

IN THIRTY-FIVE MINUTES BRIE HEADED back upstairs feeling fresh and relaxed. The hot water had melted away some of the tension that was turning her neck and shoulder muscles into tight cords. She had left her freshly washed and dried hair loose rather than returning it to the pony tail. Brie had always considered her hair to be her best feminine asset, and she may have been right, because several heads turned as she came into the kitchen.

George and Scott were just finishing drying and storing the dishes.

"All set, George?" she asked

"Yup, we're done here." He laid down his towel and followed Brie to the library where they sat down at the desk as they had that morning.

"George, I'll come right to the point. Is there anything you omitted in recounting your argument with Pete last night?"

The tic in his eye came back to life.

"The windjammer fleet is sort of a closed community," George began. "The captains all know each other, and, like any group, there's always some competition among the members. There are petty jealousies that cause rumors. I've earned a reputation over the years as the best cook in the fleet; in fact, several captains have tried to hire me. The *Sarah Trenton*, in particular, wanted me, and I think the cook aboard that ship started the rumors about me being gay." George's eye twitched uncontrollably. "I have absolutely nothing against gays, but the fact is I'm not one of them. I learned last night that Pete was a complete bigot. During our argument he told me he wouldn't work on a ship with anyone who was gay. He actually threatened me—said there was more than one way to leave the crew. His behavior was so strange I couldn't believe it. He was irrational."

Brie knew about fanatics. They can appear perfectly normal one minute and totally unbalanced the next. Hatred keeps them on the brink. Like active volcanoes, their anger may ooze out slowly, scorching everything around them, or erupt violently, without warning. She wondered if Pete could have bullied or threatened George enough to make him snap. She studied him for a moment.

"So why didn't you tell me about this when we talked this morning?" she asked.

"It's embarrassing, number one. And two, either way, gay or not, it makes me look like I had a pretty strong motive for killing Pete."

"It does do that. But it certainly helps that you've been honest." Brie's instincts were telling her that the truth and, hence, the killer, were not going to be easily discovered. She let George go, asking if he'd find Howard and send him in.

A gentle knock on the door announced Howard's arrival.

"Come in," Brie called.

Howard stepped in and closed the door. "What a beautiful library, but this isn't a good way to spend your vacation, is it?"

"I used to think I was pretty good at going with the flow," Brie said. "Lately, though, I've done a lot of paddling against the current. Anyway, thanks for your concern, Howard. Come sit down." Brie indicated the chair. "How's everybody doing today?"

"It's a subdued group, there's no doubt about that, but everyone is attempting to get along." He looked at the recorder as Brie clicked it on.

"Howard, did you see or hear anything at all unusual in the night?"

"I was so tired last night. I don't think I've ever been that tired. It may be that I'm just too old for adventures like this."

Brie noted that he hadn't addressed the question, but she decided to come back to it since his comment had presented another opportunity. "Do you do things like this with Will very often?"

"Actually, this is the first time we've ever done anything like this. I was stunned that Will wanted me to go with him. I even asked him if he wouldn't have more fun with one of his friends, but he said that I was the one he wanted on this trip with him. So, of course, I came. Will was a tag-along child—I was 46 when he was born. He was twelve years younger than his nearest sibling, and I guess we probably sheltered and spoiled him too much. By then money was no problem, but time was. I was at the peak of my career and I worked a huge number of hours."

"What was your job, Howard?"

"I owned a small manufacturing business. Anyway, I did teach Will to sail when he was young—it was the one thing we did together when he was a boy. There should have been a lot more things." Howard's eyes took on a look of regret, as if he were seeing things in focus for the first time, through the powerful lens of awareness that often only comes with age.

Suddenly, he looked up at Brie. "You know, there *was* something last night. I heard a noise in the middle of the night. It was a creaking, metallic sound. There've been lots of noises coming from the ship during the gale, but this was different from anything I'd heard. I'm not sure if it woke me up or if I happened to awake at just the right moment to hear it. It was on our side of the ship though—the starboard side. And a few moments after that I'd swear I heard someone try our door. I didn't think anything of it at the time—not knowing Pete had been murdered."

Brie thought about the position of Howard and Will's cabin. It was behind the storeroom, and the storeroom sat directly in back of the galley, separated from it by a bulkhead. Rob had checked the storeroom. Where could that sound have come from? Brie jotted the question on her note pad.

"Do you know if Will got up at all during the night?"

"Not that I know of, but if you're suggesting that he had anything to do with the murder, well, that's just impossible. Will has his problems like all of us, but he's no killer."

Spoken like a true father, Brie thought.

"I wasn't suggesting anything, Howard—just trying to account for people's whereabouts during Pete's watch."

"Of course. I'm sorry, Brie. Will has been..." Howard stopped mid-sentence and looked down at his hands.

"Will has been what?"

"Oh, nothing. Will's been having a hard summer, that's all."

Brie had the distinct feeling that Howard had started to say something entirely different and changed his mind. What could it have been? Will has been in trouble; Will has been accused of something; Will has been to jail—been arrested. What? She'd never know now.

"Why is he having a hard summer? Is it because he didn't get the job on the *Maine Wind*?"

"I think it's just entering the real world of responsibilities. No more college campus. No more having Dad foot the bill. Kids in this generation have been pretty pampered—lots of privileges and not that many responsibilities. It's a big transition for some of them."

"Well, Howard, for your sake, I hope he makes the transition smoothly. Now, I need to ask Will some questions, so why don't you send him in."

"I'll go get him, Brie," he said, rising from the chair in a manner that indicated arthritis was already a factor. He limped a step or two before his body got into the swing; then he moved with more ease toward the door and closed it quietly after himself.

Brie picked up the length of grayed rope from the desktop and swiveled around to face the window. The rain was unrelenting. She tied a bowline, untied it, and tied another. She wasn't sure she ever wanted to be a parent. There wasn't much left of most people after they got done raising kids—as if the job just chewed them up and spat them out at the other end, old and tired.

Will walked into the library without knocking. Why am I not surprised, Brie thought, turning her chair back around.

"Dad says you want to see me," he said, closing the door harder than necessary.

"Come sit down, Will."

He slouched across the room and into the chair. Throwing one leg over the arm, like he was getting ready for a bullshit session with one of his undoubtedly annoying buddies, he gave her a look that was half apathy, half arrogance. Poor Howard, Brie thought. And for that matter, poor me. Except for the surly expression, everything about Will Thackeray spelled average—medium height, medium build, medium hair color. He didn't carry himself like an athlete, but the snug fitting tee-shirt he wore revealed a well-toned body, suggesting he at least worked out.

Brie decided to play her big card first. Opening the top drawer of the desk, she took out the sock containing Pete's marline spike and laid it on the desk. "Can you explain this? I found it in your bunk this morning."

"What the hell gives you the right to go into my cabin!" He tried for indignation but totally lacked the integrity needed to carry it off.

"There's been a murder—remember? And I'm the closest thing we've got to the law. What's more, I had the captain's permission to search the ship. Now answer the question."

"I took it to make him look bad."

"Why?"

"Because he was arrogant. I thought it might bring him down a notch."

The pot and the kettle, Brie thought.

"Did you kill him for the same reason?"

"Don't be ridiculous. He wasn't worth ruining my life over."

"And did you have other plans for making him 'look bad'?"

"I guess you'll never know," he said, with an unpleasant smirk.

"Why did you keep the marline spike after Pete was murdered?"

"Souvenir. Can I have it back?"

Brie stared in disbelief. "No. It's not yours—remember?"

Will got out of his chair and headed toward the door.

"Come back and sit down," Brie ordered. She picked up her piece of rope, wrapped the two ends around her hands as they rested in her lap and snapped it tight—just in case she decided to strangle him. "You'll leave when I'm done questioning you."

She expected him to keep right on walking. But surprisingly, he stopped in his tracks, turned and slunk back to his chair.

"Why did you bring your dad with you on this cruise instead of a friend?"

Will's expression softened momentarily. "I just thought it would be nice for us to do this together. He's getting older, and …I don't know. What difference does that make?" he asked sharply, returning to his abrasive self.

Brie decided to move on. "Did you see or speak to Pete during his watch last night?"

"I saw him, although he didn't see me."

"Explain that, please." Her patience was beginning to fray.

Will took out his most obsequious smile. "I can be of some real help to you in this," he said, leaning toward her. "I saw Pete and Alyssa going at it up on deck an hour before he was found dead. And you know what else?"

"What?"

"It wasn't the first time they were up there."

"And how do you know that?"

"Let's just say I'd seen another show in the same series."

"You watched them?"

"Sure, why not—free entertainment."

Brie regarded him with distaste. *Insectavis maximus*, she thought to herself.

Will pressed on with his sordid facts.

"Last night he banged her way up in the bow of the ship. I crept along the side of the galley compartment, where it sticks up above the deck, and hid in the shadows so they couldn't see me. But I could see everything in the light from the lantern. The whole thing was so hot; they had to be so quiet—I bet that made it twice as hot." His eyes took on an unpleasant gleam. "She took off her rain slicker and she was wearing this really skimpy black dress with nothing on under it, and it got all wet in the rain. Pete pulled the top of the dress down…"

Will jabbered on but Brie was focused on two words—black dress. She hadn't seen any such garment among Alyssa's things. She guessed the dress was a figment of Will's libido-ridden imagination, but remembering the fibers under Pete's fingernails, she jotted a note to herself. There were only a few possibilities. Pete could have gotten the fibers under his fingernails in the heat of passion, Alyssa could have disposed of the dress for whatever reason, or Will could have invented the whole thing, either because he had a penchant for little black dresses or because he knew the killer had worn black.

Brie tuned back in just in time to catch the climax.

"…and then he lifted her up against the hull, she wrapped her legs around him and he took her really fast."

Will slumped back in the chair, consumed by his squalid tale.

For a moment Brie studied him through the microscope of

her disgust. She wasn't sure if he should win the prize for most odious behavior, or if it should go to Alyssa, or, posthumously, to Pete.

"Turns you on, doesn't it? Admit it," he said, with a smirk. "You're such an ice goddess—I know you've never done anything like that."

"You're right, Will. I'm a sucker for meaning in my relationships. But I'll make sure I let Rob know how much you appreciated the show. Sadly, he already knows about Alyssa, so he may as well know about you too."

Will went pale. "I was just kidding about what I said. I don't really think you're an ice goddess."

"No, Will, you're right. And, because I am, it's my duty to let Rob know the cold, hard facts. I'm done with you," she said, getting up and walking to the door. She held it open and turned to him. "Please leave."

Will got up and ducked by her. Brie knew she'd never divulge what he had described, but she secretly relished the image of Rob picking him up and breaking him in half.

She walked back to the desk, picked up her piece of rope and stepped over to the window. Rain pelted the ground outside, forming a system of miniature lakes. Now she really felt sorry for Howard, even though he may inadvertently have helped create Will's behavior. She stared out at the gloom, and as she skillfully worked the line in her hands, an elaborate Turk's head knot began to emerge. Over the past year, she'd noted in herself a diminishing capacity for tolerance. She just didn't roll with the punches the way she used to. There were more questions she should have asked Will, but she simply couldn't stand his presence any longer. She'd get back to him later, when her blood pressure had returned to normal.

Tim was the last passenger she had to interview, and she expected that to be far less eventful than dealing with Will. Tossing the Turk's head back on the desk, she opened the drawer and put away the marline spike. Stepping away from the desk she stretched her arms over her head, clasped her hands together, and leaned slowly forward, bringing her hands to the floor. She hung there for a few seconds, folded in half, and drew in several deep breaths. Then she slowly rolled back up to a standing position. Feeling a little calmer, she headed out into the hall to locate Tim.

Brie found everyone but Tim in the game room. Rob and Alyssa were playing cards, Howard was reading in the corner farthest from the TV, and John, Scott, George, and Will were watching a video with the original *Saturday Night Live* cast.

"Where's Tim?" Brie asked, looking around the room.

"He went down for a shower," Scott responded. "I was down there five minutes ago, and he still had the water running. Should I go get him?"

"If you wouldn't mind," Brie said.

Scott was back in a couple of minutes. "He's not down there. I checked the rest of the inn. He's not here."

"What! Where is he?" Brie said, her demeanor somewhere between agitated and alarmed.

Howard got up from his corner and came over. "Remember what he said last night at dinner about the trails on the island? Maybe he went for a walk."

"Without telling anyone?" There was concern in Brie's voice.

"I'll go find him, Brie," John said.

"No." Brie reached out and took hold of his forearm. "I'll go. I really need a change of scene right now. My best guess is he went up the trail behind the inn. Do you know where it leads?" she asked John.

"Through a spruce forest and over to the other side of the island, where there are some high cliffs overlooking the ocean," he replied. "I'd feel better if you let me go, though."

"I'll be fine. Stay here with the others and keep the peace."

Brie went out into the hall and collected her raincoat and rubber loafers. She walked back to the kitchen, put them on and stepped out the back door. The cold air struck her a refreshing blow. She pulled her hood up, lowered her head to avoid the direct force of the wind on her face, and headed up the path toward the woods.

She was glad to be outside. It always helped her to think, and she needed to process the information she'd gathered in the interviews. She climbed the sloping trail behind the inn and within a couple hundred yards, entered a dense spruce forest. The rain had let up temporarily, and she pushed the hood off her head so she'd have better peripheral vision in the woods. The smell of pine enveloped her and calmed her mind. She began mulling over the facts of the case as she hiked along. She knew that Rob had gone on deck very close to the time of the murder. In his interview he'd claimed to have found Pete dead. Was that the truth, or did Rob kill him? Had he actually glimpsed someone in the shadows, or had he made that up and staged both the sound Howard had heard and the trying of the door knobs to back up his story and divert suspicion from himself?

Then there was Will—dear Will. He was creepy, manipulative and a voyeur, but was he a killer? Some of his behavior was definitely beyond the normal range. Brie reviewed the murder scene in her mind. The strangulation and stabbing definitely pointed to someone with intense anger. She thought of George. Gay or not, Pete's accusations could have infuriated him far more than he'd let on. And finally Tim. What to think of Tim, with his unusual tattoo and his need to get away—to Alaska. Not a bad place to be heading if you've committed a murder in Maine.

She scanned the forest around her and up ahead to see if she could catch any movement that would indicate she was on the right track. Tim either had a good head start or he was moving quickly. Brie pressed on, tired of thinking about the murder, wanting to think about John. Wanting to think about his arms around her in the library, and how his body had felt pressed against hers.

A sudden rustling in the brush nearby snapped her to attention. Whirling around, she drew her gun. Holding it two-fisted, she turned in a 360-degree circle, scribing an arc in the air with the weapon. She squatted low to the ground, held her breath and listened. In spite of the cold her hands felt clammy, and her heart pounded in her ears. A familiar wave of anxiety—the same one that had washed over her so many times since her partner's death —turned the contents of her stomach over like pebbles on a beach. What had the doctor told her to do when this happened? She tried to remember.

Snap! Closer this time, but from a slightly different direction. Her training broke through the fog of fear and she reacted, plunging into the thicket beyond the trail and running toward a large tree ten yards away where she could take cover. Gaining the tree, she crouched down, barely breathing. Someone was out there. She could feel the presence. Watching. Waiting.

12

BRIE SQUATTED AT THE BASE of the spruce tree. Her nerves were like frayed rope, and each passing second gnawed at what was left of them. She knew she was vulnerable. She scanned the terrain for a better site. Suddenly, from where she had heard the last sound, a deer bounded out of the brush, nearly stopping her heart. She did another 360-degree scan with the pistol. No other presence seemed to have scared the deer. She slowly stood up, drew a deep breath in through her nose and slowly blew it out through her mouth. She looked up at the top of the tall spruce. "This is a forest, Brie," she said to herself. "There are animals here, and there are sounds." Gun in hand, she took large steps through the wet ground cover and made her way back to the trail, where she headed up toward the bluffs.

The trail bent to the left and up a short incline. As the wind picked up, the pine swayed and sung around her. Rhythmic booms from the other side of the island grew louder as she approached the cliffs. The deer incident had heightened her awareness, and

Brie tuned into the subtler forest sounds existing beneath the rush of wind through trees and the crash of waves against rock. Twice more she whirled around holding her breath, convinced she'd heard movement close behind her. She took it as a sign that her nerves were in no way ready to return to the department.

A few more minutes up the trail, Brie came in view of the tree line. She increased her pace and soon stepped out of the pine forest onto a granite shelf not far from the edge of the cliff. She scanned the woods to left and right for any sign of movement. The biting wind stung her hands and face. Still holding the gun, she placed her hands in her pockets to warm them up. Just beyond the tree line several gulls hung motionless in the air, riding the strong updrafts off the bluffs. Every now and then one of them would tip its wings, catching the air currents, and go soaring up into the sky.

Brie walked forward to within a foot of nothingness and looked over the edge at the thundering surf a hundred feet below. Gigantic swells driven before the northeast wind exploded against the base of the granite cliffs, throwing spray fifty feet into the air. She stood there, unswayed by the danger boiling below her, and smiled, remembering how her brother would only approach the edge of a precipice on his belly. She lingered a few moments, poised between sea and sky, at one with the watery, gray realm surrounding her. Another person might have shrunk from the violent forces on display here, but nothing in Mother Nature scared Brie half as much as what she'd seen in human nature.

She wasn't sure if it was a sound or just a feeling that registered first on her radar, but as hairs rose up on the back of her neck, her grip tightened on the pistol in her pocket. She wished she hadn't been drawn so close to the edge by the cannonading sea. The thought of whirling around and placing her back to the hundred-foot drop was paralyzing. Brie took the space of a breath to summon what calm she could and then spun around, drawing the gun. The sight snagged on the corner of her pocket, and the gun came out of her hand, hit the ground a few inches from the edge of the cliff and slid over.

Now unarmed, she faced Tim Pelletier, who stood no more than four feet from her. He appeared edgy and distracted. He studied her, a feral distrust in his eyes—eyes that were reddened either from crying or from overexposure to the strong wind.

"What are you doing here?" His tone was demanding, as if she were a trespasser in his private kingdom.

"I came looking for you. You left the inn without telling anyone." As she spoke she edged in an arc to her right, attempting to put some distance between herself and the cliff's edge.

Tim took a step forward, and Brie planted her feet, preparing for whatever might be coming. He'd seen her gun go over the edge, and she was certainly no match for him physically. His Coast Guard training would have given him many of the same self-defense skills she possessed.

"I went for a hike. Is that a crime?" His tone was aggressive, a surprising counterpoint to the demeanor she'd seen up till now.

"I shouldn't have to tell you that, because of the murder, we need to keep everyone together. Also, you're the last person I have to question, so you need to come back to the inn." As she spoke she continued her abbreviated side-stepping away from the edge.

"What *I need* is to stay up here a little longer. And anyway, there's nothing I can tell you about last night. I went to bed at 11:00 and didn't wake up until Alyssa screamed."

And there's no way to corroborate that, Brie thought. "Had you ever met Pete before coming on this cruise?"

"No, what would make you think that?" he said defensively.

"So, you met Pete for the first time when we boarded the *Maine Wind* on Friday evening?"

"That's right."

"What did you think of him?"

"At first I was pretty sure I wouldn't like him, but as I got to know him a little over the past few days, I felt differently. I don't know why, but I always feel like people are making fun of me. I didn't get that sense from Pete. I thought he was kind."

Now safely away from the edge, Brie found it easier to reflect on what Tim was saying. It was interesting—people's perceptions. She knew that George certainly didn't find Pete kind. Then she remembered Pete coming to Tim's defense last night at dinner when Will ridiculed his idea about hiking on the island. Maybe that was where Tim got his impression. Brie hugged herself to ward off the cold as she mentally sized him up. Tim's obvious insecurity about himself had led to something bordering on a persecution complex.

Brie shifted gears. "I couldn't help noticing the unusual tattoo on your chest when I bumped into you below decks this morning. You didn't mention a girlfriend when we talked at dinner last night."

Tim turned to face the ocean. "That tattoo was just a piece of youthful foolishness. The relationship ended several years ago." Regret leaked from every syllable he uttered.

"I'm sorry to hear that, Tim."

"No big deal."

"Why don't we head back to the inn now?" Brie nodded in the direction of the trail as she spoke. "We can finish talking there —it'll be a lot warmer."

A guarded look returned to Tim's eyes. "I need to be up here a little longer."

"And I need you to return to the group," Brie said. But short of marching him back at gunpoint—now an impossibility—she could see that she wasn't going to prevail.

"I'll head back in fifteen minutes. Okay?"

"Fine. Fifteen minutes." She wasn't going to win this round, and she didn't intend to stand any longer in the raw wind trying to face him down. She turned and strode toward the woods, disappearing into the darkness of the forest.

John had just stepped out of the bathroom when he heard the phone. He headed for the library and caught it on the fourth ring. "Snug Harbor Bed and Breakfast," he said.

"This is Garrett Parker calling for Brie Beaumont."

"She's stepped out for a few minutes. Can I take a message? This is John DuLac, captain of the *Maine Wind*."

"Stepped out where? I thought she was on an island in the middle of a gale."

"She went after one of the passengers who decided to take a walk."

"By herself?"

"That's how she wanted it. I told her I'd rather go, but she refused my offer."

"By herself!" Garrett said again. "Haven't you ever heard of backup?"

John smelled a fight in the making. "Look, I'm a sailor, not a cop. I'm not going to tell Brie how to do her job—she's the detective."

"Brie's been through a lot in the past year. She doesn't need any more trouble."

"In her line of work there'll always be trouble. What Brie needs is to find her confidence again."

"Right," said Garrett. "And she'll have the best chance of doing that back here at the department. If you care about her, you should encourage her to return home."

"Brie's at a crossroads in her life. She needs to decide whether to hold her course or come about and try a different tack."

"Spoken like a true sea captain," Garrett said, his hostility mounting. "You're such an authority on what Brie needs—how long have you known her?" he asked.

John was silent. He wasn't about to admit that he'd known

her for only five days. "Hmmm, my detective skills are telling me it's probably less than a month. Right?"

"Your detective skills be damned. Brie doesn't need you or me to make up her mind for her. Time will do that nicely, and she's made a wise choice to give herself plenty of that." This conversation was escalating into all-out war, and John decided to call for a cease fire. "Look, Garrett, Brie should be back in a few minutes and I'll have her call you. All right?"

"Fine, and don't forget—I have some information that may help her."

John hung up the phone and walked over to the big window behind the desk. The conversation had brought the strength of his feelings for Brie into sharp focus, and he was forced to look at them. At 39, he had known his share of women, but none of them had held the fascination that Brie did for him. She was smart, pretty, and she had character too. He decided to face the possibility that he might be falling in love with her. What was more—Garrett's pontificating aside—he was going to try his darnedest to keep her in Maine a while longer so things might have a chance to develop between them. He planned to ask her if she'd take Pete's job and stay aboard the *Maine Wind* for the summer. After all, she was a veteran sailor with all the necessary qualifications, and what she didn't know he'd teach her. He knew Will would want the job now, but Will was just too negative and arrogant, and there'd already been enough crew problems for this season.

John headed back to the game room where George had just set down a steaming bowl of buttered popcorn and a large pot of hot cocoa. In spite of the circumstances George was doing his best to pamper the passengers and raise their spirits a bit. It seemed to be working—there was actually some joking about putting on an aerobics video to work off the popcorn after they were done.

The sound of a pickup truck drew John to the window. Glenn was just pulling up in front of the inn. John headed for the front door to meet him.

"Glenn, this is a surprise. What's up?"

"I would have called, but the phone lines were down on the other side of the island, and I thought it was important enough to drive over here."

"Let's go into the living room where we'll have some privacy," John said. At that moment they heard the back door of the inn open and close. "Let's make that the kitchen, Glenn. I think that's Brie just coming back in."

They found her in the kitchen, ruddy cheeked, shaking the water off her raincoat. "Any sign of Tim?" John asked.

"I found him, but he wanted another fifteen minutes by himself, and there was no way of forcing the issue." She couldn't bring herself to tell John about the gun. It made her look like the bumbling detective—definitely not her M.O. until now. "Glenn, what brings you back to the inn?" she asked, walking over to the coffee and pouring herself a mug.

"I was telling John the phone lines are down, and Betty remembered something I thought might be important. She was convinced that there was something familiar about Pete's name, and she finally remembered. She's pretty sure he worked for a lobster fisherman here on the island a few years ago. She thinks it was Jack Trudeau."

"Is this Jack Trudeau still on the island?" Brie asked.

"Yup. Keeps his boat down in the cove when he's not out working his traps."

"I'm going down there and see if I can find him," Brie said. "Do you know if he lives in the village, Glenn?"

"His is one of the last houses at the far end of town. Ask anyone down there—they'll direct you. You might try his boat first, though."

"Will do." She took a large swig of her coffee to fortify herself against the cold wind and headed over to collect her coat and rubber loafers. She walked with John and Glenn to the front door. "John, if Tim's not back within ten minutes, send Scott after him.

Okay?" She put on her coat and shoes, and was just turning the knob when John remembered Garrett's call and told her about it.

"Maybe you should call him before you leave. He seemed eager to talk to you—said he had some information." John refrained from telling her what a snit Garrett was in about her leaving the inn alone.

"I've been waiting for his call. I'd better take care of it now." She took her coat and shoes back off. But before heading to the library, she walked back over to Glenn and gave his forearm an affectionate squeeze. "Thanks for bringing me the information, Glenn."

As she padded down the hall, Glenn turned to John. "I have to go," he said placing a hand on John's shoulder. "I promised Betty I'd get right back." They walked out onto the porch together, and after the door was closed Glenn said, "You know, John, I really like that girl—she's got something special."

"I know," John said wistfully. "Me too."

In the library, Brie picked up the receiver and punched in Garrett's number. He answered on the second ring. "Homicide division—Parker speaking."

"Garrett—it's Brie. John said you called."

"Brie! What are you doing traipsing around that island by yourself with a killer on the loose?"

"Take it easy, Gare. There's this thing called an off-duty gun— I carry it just in case." As she spoke she unclipped the empty holster from her waist and put it in the top drawer with her fanny pack.

"Well, just be careful—okay? By the way, it sounds like the captain is falling for you."

"Don't be ridiculous, Gare, we've only known each other for five days."

"Five days," Garrett guffawed. "Wow, I way overestimated."

"What are you talking about?"

"I told him he'd probably known you less than a month. But five days—that's rich."

"I wouldn't worry about it, Gare. I've dealt with killers—I think I can handle one sea captain."

"Well, just be careful where you're handling him, Brie. That guy's in love with you, and you need to make a break for it or you'll end up chained to the stove in his galley."

"Oh, really! And you want me back at the department to make coffee. So who's the bigger chauvinist?"

"You're a city girl, Brie. Come home where you belong." Garrett sounded ticked off now.

"So, did you call just to give advice to the lovelorn, or have you come up with something useful?"

"I ran a thorough check on all the names you gave me and came up with nothing but a few traffic violations, until I got to Will Thackeray."

"What did you find on him?" she asked.

"He's from a small town—Pawcatuck, Connecticut—now there's a mouthful. There was an incident when Thackeray was a senior in high school. Even though no formal charges were filed, the sheriff remembered the case well. Apparently Will Thackeray threatened the life of a fellow student after losing a wrestling match to him during the state championships that year. The parents of the threatened student put a lot of pressure on the high school to expel Will. The school finally agreed to let him graduate with the condition that he undergo a psychological profile."

"Did you get the results of the profile?" Brie asked.

"The report stated that parts of the test were inconclusive; still, the diagnosis read possible borderline schizophrenia."

"Wow! Anything else?"

"I called the high school and found out where Will attended college. The college had no record of any incidents involving Thackeray, but, interestingly, he was never involved in sports during his four years there. Apparently he stuck strictly to academics. Graduated magna cum laude. I hope it's some help."

Brie's mind had inadvertently wandered back to the "captain's in love with you" statement.

"Brie? You there?"

"I'm here," she said, trying to refocus. "You can be the judge, Gare. We've got a situation here where the murdered man beat Will out for a summer job aboard the windjammer that I'm sailing on—a job Will desperately wanted."

"Interesting. What's your gut telling you?"

"He's arrogant, and I believe emotionally unstable. From what you've told me he could be dangerous. Listen, Gare, I've gotta go. There's another lead I have to follow up on. Thanks a lot for your help."

"Be careful, Brie, and come home."

"Talk to you soon, Gare." She hung up. She thought about his concern and decided it bordered on jealousy. That didn't make any sense, though. She and Garrett had known each other for almost four years, and they were good friends but no more. Obviously there was something he *didn't* know about her, and that was the more he pushed one way, the more she'd push the other. The one thing she'd managed to keep from being sucked into the whirlpool of emotional chaos was her independence. She often felt it was her only lifeline to her former self, so she clung to it like a drowning victim, believing she might yet pull herself to safety. Brie headed back toward the front door and donned her coat and shoes.

John stepped into the hall to talk to her before she left, and he noted the quizzical look she gave him. No doubt Garrett had felt compelled to shoot off his big mouth about their heated conversation. Without commenting, he opened the front door and they stepped out onto the porch.

"I'll be back as soon as I can," Brie said, heading for the steps.

John started to follow her, but then stopped himself. She seemed in a rush to get away from him, and before he could speak she was off the porch, moving across the lawn toward the road. He watched her go. Long ribbons of blond hair escaped her hood, blowing out behind her in the strong wind. His throat felt tight—crammed full of words he longed to speak but didn't know how.

13

ONCE ON THE ROAD, BRIE MOVED at a swift pace to counteract the chill wind. The exercise felt good. Her muscles were still warm from the hike up to the bluffs, and as she walked, her fingers began to tingle indicating her heart was pumping at a good rate. Her list of questions was growing longer with each interview. The walk down to the village would give her time to sort things out. She thought about her encounter with Tim up on the cliff. By catching him off guard, she'd gotten a glimpse of a part of him he kept well hidden. Something tormented him. What was it? And did it relate to the murder?

Then there was the information Garrett had turned up about Will and the psychological profile. It confirmed her feeling that Will was unstable. He was also physically capable of killing Pete. He had a wrestling background, and while his motive didn't seem strong enough, maybe coupled with his emotional instability it was. And now, the news that Pete may have worked on the island. Another interesting twist. Funny he hadn't mentioned living on the island when Tim talked about the hiking trails last night.

Brie quickened her pace, which had started to lag as she mulled over the case. She was surprised at how good the routine of conducting the investigation felt. The process of sifting through facts and motives had a comfortable familiarity, like a well-broken-in pair of shoes. Maybe I'm ready to go home, she thought. *But then again, this is different from back home. There I'm just a cog in a big city homicide division.* She realized she enjoyed directing this investigation. Perhaps she'd like working for a police department in a smaller community, or maybe even as a private investigator.

"City girl. *Not.* I may have always lived in a big city, but there's a part of me that would leave that life in an instant," she said to the trees that lined the gravel road. Stress, noise, crime, traffic. She wasn't like some of her friends in the department who thrived on the night life of the city. She liked to find her adventure in the great outdoors, not in a downtown bar. In her day to day routine, curling up in her pajamas with a good book and a glass of wine was more her style. She'd always been driven when it came to her job, but that was more a product of her own self-expectations than love of any particular work environment. Which raised another issue she'd been struggling with.

From a young age she'd been taught to strive for excellence. Only recently had she begun to wonder if, in that striving, she hadn't allowed enough room for error—for the inevitability of her own human error. Over the last few months she'd also thought a lot about accidents, and she was learning to view them with a kind of neutrality. That they happen, that they are part of life, and that someone isn't necessarily responsible for them, were all possibilities she'd begun to consider. In her work Brie was always searching for reasons—motives, always probing behind the seemingly accidental for the truth—the cause. Away from her work, for the first time in years, she'd begun to think differently about lots of things. Maybe there just wasn't a reason or a cause for everything. And if that were the case, maybe someday she could forgive herself for Phil. Maybe she couldn't have prevented his death. Since that terrible night she'd believed *she* was the cause. She'd reviewed the scene in her mind a thousand times, finding a thousand ways to blame herself.

Brie had reached the bottom of the hill and headed into the village of Lobsterman's Cove. A few houses and a white steeple church lined the road at this end of the village. One gray-shingled house caught her attention. It had a sign suspended from the front porch railing that read *Mabel and Melvin's Haircuts for All*. Brie smiled wondering whether it was a mom and pop barber shop, or if Mabel and Melvin were just two acquaintances who decided to set up shop together. She'd just passed the general store and headed down a fork in the road running around the east side of the cove where most of the lobsterboats were moored, when she heard a screen door bang and a voice enthusiastically hail her.

"Miss Beaumont, is that you? Miss Beaumont!"

Brie turned and suppressed a smile as she saw bobble-headed Fred Klemper steaming toward her. In the midst of all the human and meteorologic grimness Fred provided a welcome comic relief. He reminded her of the Road Runner, maybe because of his long, thin neck and the forward pitch to his walk. He tilted dangerously as he loped toward her, so that at any moment Brie expected him to stub his toe and go sailing into the waters of the cove.

"Hello, Fred," she said as he lurched safely to a stop in front of her. She was fully prepared for a detailed update on "the body."

"Miss Beaumont, I saw you walking along and, well, I just thought you might wanna check on the body." The end of his sentence was punctuated with nods.

"I'm sure you're giving it the best of care in your cooler, Fred. And by the way, you can call me Brie."

He looked at his shoes in an "aw shucks" kind of way, and his cheeks turned a rosy pink, as if she'd just made a pass at him. She seriously hoped her offer of informality hadn't been misconstrued.

"The captain's very grateful for your help, Fred. I'll let him know that you're staying on top of the situation."

His deflated chest puffed up, and he looked at her shyly through thick glasses. "Glad to be of help—I've always liked Captain DuLac."

"Maybe you could help *me* right now, Fred. I'm looking for Jack Trudeau. Do you know which of the boats down there is his?" she asked, gesturing toward the cove.

"The one with the black hull, tied up at the last dock. Down the end of the road there," he said, raising a scarecrow arm and pointing across the cove. "He's a rough character, though. You watch your step, Miss Beaumont. Maybe you should bring Captain DuLac with you."

"I'll be okay, Fred. By the way, the man who was murdered— Pete McAllister—do you remember him working here on the island a few years ago?"

"Can't say for sure. Might have, I guess." Fred suddenly appeared uncomfortable. He buried his hands in his pockets and looked at the ground. "Gotta get back now," he said abruptly, his head resuming its familiar motion. "Business to take care of, you know." Without looking at her he turned and, maintaining his previous angle of trajectory, rushed back toward his store.

"See you later, Fred." She smiled after him. They certainly broke the mold, she thought.

Brie wondered about Fred's apparent discomfort at discussing Pete's employment on the island. John had told her the islanders could be tightlipped with outsiders, but she sensed there was something else going on with Fred. He appeared to be intimidated by Jack Trudeau. Maybe even frightened. And he was certainly reluctant to discuss anything that might relate to him.

The north wind tugged at Brie as she moved away from the shelter of the hill and walked down toward the cove. The tide was high, and a number of lobsterboats bobbed up and down next to the wooden docks. Rain had turned the road into a mud hole. She skirted the edge of it, avoiding the mucky ground. Toward the end of the road she crossed over, headed down a small flight of wooden stairs and walked out the dock toward Trudeau's boat. As she approached she caught the smell of pipe tobacco on the carrying wind.

Pausing beside the boat, she called out, "Ahoy, there." A tree of a man stepped out of the wheel house, pipe in hand. Brie judged him to be somewhere in his mid-thirties. He was easily 6'4" and broad as the beam of his lobsterboat. A mass of curly black hair covered his head, buffering the impact of his hard blue eyes.

"I'm looking for Jack Trudeau," Brie said.

"You found him." The eyes roamed over her.

"Permission to come aboard?"

"Come ahead." As she stepped over the gunwale and into the boat, Brie could feel him weighing and measuring every inch of her.

"You must be the pretty detective everyone's talking about. You're stirring up more interest than that body up in Klemper's store." There was an edge to his voice as cold as the north Atlantic. "I figured you'd get around to me before long."

"I'm told Pete McAllister worked for you a few years ago."

Trudeau stepped uncomfortably close to her, but Brie held her ground on the gently rolling deck, and met his gaze with a distillate of pure grit and defiance she'd formulated over twelve years of dealing with tough, often intimidating men. Sensing that her borders were well guarded, Trudeau took a step back, removed the pipe from his mouth, and answered in a tone tinged with respect.

"Pete McAllister was my sternman for a couple seasons. I let him go three years ago during a bad season. Lobsters just dried up that year. Couldn't afford to pay him." He took a long pull from his pipe and watched her.

"So, he lived here on the island during that time?" Brie asked.

"That's right. Rented a little cabin up the east shore from

here." Trudeau jabbed with his pipe stem toward the island. "More of a shack, really—just two small rooms and a privy out back. Guess he liked the seclusion."

"Was he a good worker?"

"Worked hard enough. It's a backbreaking job, sternman is."

"Did he ever have any trouble with anyone here on the island?" Brie waited for his reaction.

Trudeau watched a seagull wheel and land on the choppy water. "McAllister was more interested in his rock climbing than befriending anyone here on the island. He'd have a few drinks up at the Two Claws Bar on occasion. But mostly kept to himself. There was no trouble." He put the pipe back in his mouth.

"He had a reputation as a womanizer," Brie said, observing the lobsterman closely. "Was he involved with anyone here on the island?"

Trudeau drilled his eyes into her with such intensity that Brie felt pressure on the back of her skull. "He took the ferry to the mainland most weekends—taught rock climbing over there, I heard. Did his womanizing over there too, I'd guess." His voice was flat, emotionless, unreadable, but Brie felt a familiar vibration in her gut which always told her one of two things—be careful or dig deeper in this spot. Trudeau continued, "After the accident he moved away. Was gone within two weeks."

"Accident?" Surprise came before Brie could mask it. "What happened?"

"McAllister had brought a group of rock climbers he knew over from the mainland. They were going to scale the cliffs on the other end of the island. A girl died that day—girl from Rockland. It was all over the papers. Something went wrong when she was near the top of the cliff. She fell. Name was Megan or Marilyn—something like that but more unusual." He took a deliberate pull from his pipe and watched her.

"It would help if you could remember the name," Brie encouraged.

His brows knit together in an attempt to recover the lost name, and he studied the deck planks underfoot as if it might be written there. Suddenly he brightened. "Madeleine—that was it. Her name was Madeleine. Can't remember the last name, though."

The name meant nothing to Brie, but there was a chance it might to someone back at the inn. She thanked Trudeau and climbed onto the dock, conscious of his eyes on her. She was about to leave when a final question occurred to her. Turning back around, she found herself at eye level with the black-haired goliath. "Are you married, Jack?" she asked.

A hint of amusement momentarily warmed the steely eyes. "No, but if you're interested I'd be glad to let you sample the goods." His eyes did a lascivious scan of her raincoat, pausing at all the appropriate places.

"Ever *been* married?" Brie asked, ignoring his lewdness.

"Never found anyone worth giving up my freedom for as yet." Trudeau took a step forward, closing the gap between them. Brie felt his raw lust engulf her. He spoke in a husky voice. "I'd trade my freedom pretty quick for the thrill of hearin' *you* beggin' me for it every night."

Brie didn't miss a beat. "That sounds something like a proposal, Jack. But I'm afraid I have to return to my job in downtown Minneapolis." She stepped even closer to him and spoke seductively. "If you're interested, though, we could get a little apartment right on the bus line near police headquarters, and I'll bet you could find some work in a grocery store nearby—maybe something dealing with seafood."

Trudeau staggered back, as if the repellent thought had smacked him square between the eyes. "No thanks," he stammered. "I'd be lost without the sea. I'm sure you'll find a nice fellow to live on the bus line with you though."

Brie shrugged as if his lack of interest mystified her. Then she turned and walked off the dock, retracing her steps back along the road. She had passed two docks when she heard a voice call, "Hello there." Turning, she saw a young woman hailing her from the back of a lobsterboat. Brie immediately reversed course and headed out the dock, greeting the woman with a wave. As a detective, she'd learned to seize any opportunity that presented itself, and she hoped this one might offer yet another perspective on Pete's time here. As she neared the end of the dock, Brie recognized the woman's face. She was the same person who'd been looking out the window at them when they carried the body up to Fred's store, her shyness of this morning obviously ousted by curiosity.

"You must be the detective that's sailing on the *Maine Wind*," she said when Brie was within ten feet of the boat.

"Word travels fast around here, doesn't it?" Brie said, smiling.

"Sure does. And believe me, once Fred Klemper knows something, the rest of the village will find out within fifteen minutes."

Brie found her jovial nature a relief after dealing with Jack Trudeau.

"Why don't you come aboard and have a cup of coffee? Wind's like a knife today—goes right through you."

"Thanks," said Brie. "That'd be great." She stepped over the gunwale into the boat and followed the woman into the wheel house.

"Name's Anna Marie Stevens," she said, sitting down on a wooden crate and pouring coffee from an old black thermos into a battered metal cup she'd set on the floor of the wheel house. "And this is my boat—*Just Jake*." Anna said it with warmth in her voice like one introducing a close friend. "She was my dad's boat. Jake was his name—grandpa's too. When he died two years ago, I took 'er over. Took over his traps too." She poured the second dose into the thermos top, screwed the stopper back in place, and handed the metal cup to Brie.

"Thanks for your hospitality," Brie said. She pulled up a second crate Anna had pointed to and introduced herself. "I'm Brie Beaumont."

"I was keeping an eye on you over there." She nodded toward Trudeau's boat. "Jack can be unpredictable."

"Thanks for that," Brie said. "I'm tougher than I look, though. You run into your fair share of ones like him in my line of work."

She studied Anna, who was, without a doubt, the prettiest lobster fisherman she'd ever meet. Her tanned skin set off a pair of spring green eyes, and her long, thick hair, tangled from the strong wind, was as black and wild as a storm wave at night. "I'm surprised people are down on their boats today—the weather's so bad." Brie took a large swallow of coffee and her eyebrows went up with surprise. "This is good!"

"I can't deal with bad weather *and* bad coffee," Anna joked. "I'm just cleanin' up the boat a little. This storm's gonna break by morning, and I wanna head out early. It's too bad about Pete McAllister," she said, shifting the topic, undoubtedly driven by her curiosity. "What's gonna happen with his body?"

"The Coast Guard will pick it up as soon as they can get here." Brie looked out at the nodding lobster boats. "Did you know Pete very well? I'm told he lived here for two years."

"He was friendly enough but didn't have much interest in the locals. Word went around that he was trying to break into the lobster business—maybe hoping to get his own boat someday. The boat's only about ten percent of it, though. You need a territory and, believe me, they're closely guarded. You pretty much have to inherit one to make it in this business."

"I'm sure it's no secret that Pete was a womanizer. Did you or anyone you know ever date him?"

"Pete left here most weekends. There was one girl he cozied up to when he first got here, but she and her parents moved away. I heard he liked the submissive type though, and, well, that's just not me. You gotta be tough to make it in this business. Dad raised me to stand on my own. I could never play games with any man. Someday I'll find the right guy, but he'll have to take me the way I am—lobsterboat and all."

Brie admired Anna's spunk and wouldn't have minded passing a little more time with her, but she needed to get back to the inn. Something was bugging her, picking around the edges of her brain. Something about Pete and the rock climbing accident, but she couldn't put her finger on what it was. Now she knew why he hadn't mentioned living on the island. A girl had died on his climb—he probably felt responsible. She finished her last swallow of coffee, stood up and thanked Anna for her time. Leaving her in the wheel house, Brie walked to the stern of the boat, stepped up on the dock, and headed back toward the village.

Her encounter with Trudeau ran through her mind as she moved briskly along the road and started up the hill toward the inn. His desire for her had struck some repellent yet fascinating chord, and it played on her, eventually transposing itself to another key. She increased her pace in an attempt to clear her head, but it was suddenly full of the thought, the image, the very scent of John DuLac. And Garrett's words: "Sounds like the captain's falling for you." Desire clung to her, fogging her mind. DuLac had somehow managed to make his way under her skin, and his presence there, coupled with the brisk walk up the hill, was pushing beads of sweat up through her pores, making her layers of clothing suddenly uncomfortable. She wondered if this uncontrolled desire was a healthy thing—a sign of recovery—or a sign that she was losing it completely.

"Snap out of it, Brie," she scolded herself loudly. She stopped in her tracks, unzipped her raincoat and turned to face the raw wind. "Now, focus," she told herself. She thought again of Trudeau's account of the accident, and the name he'd assigned to the dead girl. Madeleine. Something about that name. What was it? Why did it ring some distant bell in her consciousness?

"Think, Brie. Madeleine—Elaine—Adelaide—Mad—*Maddening*—Madie. Madie!" It struck her like a hard slap. She'd seen that name just this morning. It was tattooed across Tim's chest underneath a rising sun. Madie. Could it be a coincidence? Made-

138

leine—Madie. No way.

Pieces began to fall into place. The tattoo, the name, and the picture she'd seen in Tim's cabin of the group of young people. There were packs and ropes on the ground—climbing equipment. And the wild look in Tim's eyes when she'd encountered him on the bluffs. His need to stay there and the anguish in his voice when he spoke about the relationship that had ended. Tim's girl, the one the sun rose and set in, had died up on the cliffs that day. Died on the climb that Pete was in charge of. Oh, motive, sweet motive, Brie thought. But her exuberance was short-lived as another thought immediately registered on her radar. She took off at a dead run up the hill. Two breathless minutes later she rounded a sharp turn in the road and nearly collided with John. She skidded to a stop as he caught her in his arms.

"God, you scared me," she said, stepping back. She bent over from the waist, placing her hands on her knees, and gulped in air, trying to recover from the jog up the hill.

"I thought I'd better come find you. Tim hasn't returned to the inn—I sent Scott out to look for him, but no luck. What's more, Will managed to sneak out."

"What!" Brie came to attention.

"I said Will snuck out of the inn."

"How?" Brie demanded in a February-in-Minnesota tone of voice.

"He went down to take a shower not too long after you left. I'd been down once to check on him—make sure he was still down there—and when I came up the phone rang. I grabbed it in the library, and when I came out a few minutes later Will was nowhere to be found. I immediately sent Scott after him."

"Did he find him?"

"Yup, he was heading back toward the inn. Said he wanted to get a little exercise."

"Yeah, right, I'll believe that when mooses fly. He's the laziest, whiniest excuse for a human I've encountered in a long time."

"I think it's moose," John said.

"What?"

"I think it's just moose—you said 'mooses.' I think moose is the plural too."

"*Really*. Well, thank you for that, Mr. Grammarian. Now, if you could just be that conscientious about policing the showers, we wouldn't have to keep retrieving people."

"Sorry, Brie. I admit I've never been good at bathroom patrol. In grade school I always got in trouble for letting too many boys in there at once. And you're starting to remind me of this one nun..."

Brie held her hands up in surrender. "Okay, enough," she said, suppressing a smile. "We have to find Tim. *Now*. So where did Scott look?"

"After he brought Will back to the inn, I sent him out again to get Tim. Will said he'd seen Tim near the cliffs, so Scott headed up there. When he didn't find him, he checked a couple of adjoining trails—one that drops down toward the village and another one that runs toward the western side of the island. After about forty minutes he came back to the inn to see if Tim had returned. I told him to stay with the rest of the group while I went to find you."

"Come on. We've gotta hurry."

"Where are we going?"

"I just hope we're not too late," she called back. She was already jogging up the remainder of the road.

They rounded the inn without stopping, heading for the trail that wound up to the bluffs. Once in the woods their jog was reduced to a brisk hike due to the uneven ground. Brie's body was damp from the exertion. She wished she'd waited on that shower. Finally she shed her raincoat, laying it by the side of the trail. "I'll get it on the way back," she said. Within ten minutes they stepped out of the woods onto bare granite and looked around. There was no sign of Tim. Drawn by the sound of the pounding surf, Brie walked toward the edge of the cliff.

"Brie!" John caught up with her and grabbed her by the wrist. "Be careful—there's loose rock."

"It's okay, John. I'm not a child you need to keep well in hand."

"Just be careful, okay?" he said, moving back from the edge.

He's not too keen on heights, she thought. Stepping cautiously up to the very brink, she looked over. Her fears were confirmed. Death floated a hundred feet below. Tim's body bobbed face down in the surf, held captive by a group of boulders that kept his body from being carried away on the undertow.

"He went off the cliff, John. He's dead." She stared down, as if mesmerized by the scene below.

John stepped up beside her and looked over. "My God, Brie, what could have happened? Do you think he slipped?"

"I think it's more likely he jumped," she replied. "I believe he killed Pete to avenge the death of his girlfriend, Madie. I learned from Jack Trudeau that she died here on a rock-climbing outing Pete was leading."

"I remember the story about that girl's death." John watched the sea surging far below. "It was in the papers two or three years ago. Pete's name had to have been there too, but it never rang a bell when I hired him."

"It's not that surprising, John. You deal with lots of people and lots of names every season."

Brie stepped back a few feet and was studying the ground for any signs of a struggle, when the ghost of a movement drew her attention to the edge of the woods. As she approached, she saw it was a piece of paper. Caught in the brush near the ground, it flapped erratically up and down.

John was lying on his stomach looking over the edge of the cliff, trying to decide the best course of action for recovering the body, when Brie hailed him. Carefully getting up from his prone position, he made his way over to her. The damp rag of paper she handed him had a notch torn from the top as if it might have been nailed to a tree. In blue printing Tim had penned his final words:

Pete had to die because he took Madie away.
Now my only peace is with her. I'm sorry.

14

BRIE AND JOHN HIKED DOWN the narrow trail toward the inn. Several silent minutes passed before either of them was willing to talk about the next move.

Brie finally broke the silence. "How will we retrieve the body?" she asked.

"We can't get to it by boat, the waves are too high. We'd be smashed on the rocks. I'll radio the Coast Guard when we get back and see if they can't get to us before dark, but my guess is we'll have to deal with this. There's a rescue harness on the ship for retrieving a man from the water. One of us will have to go down the cliff after the body. Scott's the best choice—he's used to working up high on the masts. We'll rig up the boson's sling to a rope and pulley. With a few of us on top of the cliff, we shouldn't have any trouble hauling the body up."

"I guess Fred will have to make room for one more body," Brie said, imagining what his reaction might be. "That cooler's really filling up. I don't know if he'll be able to stand the excitement." Like many cops, Brie tended toward black humor in moments of stress.

"He'll have a story to tell," John said. "Everybody should have at least one really good one."

They tramped on in silence for a couple of minutes. "If you want you can stay at the inn with Alyssa and Howard when we go up after the body."

"I should really be there to examine the body when it first comes up. But I see no problem with leaving Howard and Alyssa at the inn. She's so distraught she certainly doesn't need to see another body. And Howard is very fatherly—he'll keep an eye on her."

"Sounds like a plan. You know, Brie, my shakedown cruise has turned into the cruise from hell. When word of the murder gets out, and it will, I'll be hard pressed to fill my summer schedule. The cancellations will come flying in like geese on the migration."

"I'm sorry, John."

"Maybe I could coin a new slogan for my mailing piece," he said cynically. "Sail with DuLac—you may never go back."

Rain began to fall. Brie donned her raincoat, which she'd reclaimed from the side of the trail on the way down. "I have a confession to make," she said suddenly.

"Oh?"

"My gun fell over the cliff when I went up to find Tim the first time."

"Really?" he responded uncertainly.

"Just thought I'd tell you. And you know what's funny?"

"I could use some humor. What?"

"I don't even care. Which isn't normal. Normally, I'd beat myself up for at least five years over one like that. I spent so many years trying to be the perfect cop, and what did it get me? My partner's dead, and I went through something not far from a nervous breakdown. So much for perfection."

John remained silent.

"Don't you see?" Brie pressed on. "Something in me has

changed." There was a note of happiness in her voice. "Something has changed—and I think I like it."

"Maybe the Maine air agrees with you," John said hopefully.

"Maybe." They emerged from the woods and within a minute stepped in the back door of the inn. They shed their coats and shoes and headed toward the front of the inn. "I'll share the sad news with the others if you want to radio the Coast Guard," Brie said.

"Okay. I'll be down in a couple minutes and send Scott and George to the ship for what we need."

She stopped for a moment, placing a hand on his arm. "At least we can let our guard down a little now, since all the evidence suggests that Tim killed Pete. When we get back to the ship I'll look for a sample of his handwriting that I can compare with the note we found. My guess is they'll match. Considering how he was up on the bluffs this afternoon, I think it's a safe bet this was a suicide. I just wish I hadn't left him there. I should have tried harder to bring him back. I wish I'd had an inkling about Madie."

"It's not your fault, Brie. If he was determined to kill himself, I don't know if anyone could have stopped him."

Brie checked her watch as she headed for the game room— 5:45. At least they had plenty of time to get the equipment from the ship and recover the body before dusk. Everyone but Howard and Scott was in the game room. She found the two of them reading in the library and asked them to join the others.

"I'm afraid I have some distressing news." She paused, grateful there was no relative or friend of Tim's here to receive the blow. The one truly terrible part of her work was breaking the news of violent death to a victim's loved ones. "I'm sorry to have to tell you this, but Tim is dead. It appears he murdered Pete, and then committed suicide."

"Where is he? What happened?" Will asked, more out of morbid curiosity than any genuine concern, Brie guessed.

"The captain and I found his body at the foot of the cliffs on the other side of the island. I believe he jumped to his death."

"Oh, no," Alyssa sobbed, burying her face in Rob's chest. "It's so horrible. This is all so horrible." Rob rocked her in his arms.

"If there's any comfort I can offer, it's that maybe you can all sleep a little easier tonight."

As she was finishing, the captain entered. "I've notified the Coast Guard. They're still responding to distress calls from the gale, but they hope to be here by noon tomorrow. We're going to have to recover Tim's body."

"Where will the Coast Guard take the bodies?" Howard asked.

"They'll bring them back to the Coast Guard station and turn them over to the coroner. Weather permitting, we'll sail for the mainland tomorrow. I'm sorry things have turned out this way. I'll see to it that everyone receives a refund for the last half of the cruise."

Rob spoke up. "We're not worried about that, Captain. None of this is your fault."

Surprise crossed John's face. "Thanks, Rob," he said.

In the last eight hours Brie had actually started to like Rob. She was guarded about those feelings, though. The change in his demeanor had been sudden and dramatic, like the San Andreas fault in some seismic shift.

"Scott," DuLac said, turning to him. "I'm sending you and George back to the ship for equipment. Rob, I need you to go with them and help carry some of the gear, if you wouldn't mind."

"That's fine, Captain."

John produced a piece of paper and pen he'd brought from upstairs and started writing a list as he talked. "We'll need the bosun's sling, the rescue harness, the 300-foot length of rope, the blocks that suspend the yawl boat, a short length of the braided nylon line that we can run around a tree and attach to one of the blocks, the second backboard, a tarp, rope for lashing, and a roll of duct tape. And Scott, put on your wet suit. You're going to be in the water when we lower you down there. Make it as quick as you can, okay?"

"Aye, Captain."

The three men headed out into the hall to put on their raincoats. Brie heard the front door open and close after them.

She walked over to where John was standing. "I'm going to grab a cup of coffee and talk to Will in the library for a few minutes. I want to find out if he got up as far as the bluffs when he left the inn. If he saw Tim up there, he might have something to add."

John nodded. "Sounds good. I'll stay here with the others. I'm expecting Glenn and Betty to arrive back soon. We'll need to use Glenn's truck to get the body down to the village."

Brie walked over to where Will was shooting a solitary game of pool. "I need to talk to you in the library for a few minutes," she said, expecting a dose of his antagonism. She was surprised when he set down his cue without comment and followed her out of the room. She wondered if two deaths in two days was enough to sober even Will.

Brie stopped by the kitchen for coffee and then ushered Will into the library and over to the corner where Howard and Scott had been reading.

"The captain told me you left the inn this afternoon while I was down in the village." Brie sat down across from him. "Where did you think you were going, and why did you sneak out?"

"I didn't sneak out." Surliness returned to his voice. "I just walked out. Tim did the same thing, so what's the big deal?"

"The big deal is that I told everyone they had to stay together."

"Well, I just went for a walk. That's not a crime, is it?"

Brie wasn't about to qualify his wisecrack with an answer.

"Scott ran into you on the trail that leads up to the bluffs," she said. "Did you get all the way to the top of the trail?"

Will hesitated, as if unsure of what he wanted to disclose.

"Will, did you see Tim up there?"

"Yes."

"Did the two of you talk?"

"Briefly."

"Can you elaborate, please?"

"I was impressed by the view and the height of the cliffs. The waves were tremendous. It sounded like a cannon firing when they exploded against the rock. I told him he was right about what he said last night. That it was quite a place. He seemed irritated somehow. Asked what I was doing there. Like it was his own private spot or something. I told him I wanted to stretch my legs, and since he thought he could leave the group, I decided I could too. He just turned his back to me and walked over toward the edge of the cliff and stood there, looking off. I yelled to him—told him he shouldn't get so close to the edge. But he just stood there like he didn't hear me." The surliness ebbed from Will's eyes. "I know I rub people the wrong way sometimes, but I wasn't rude to him. If I'd thought he was getting ready to jump off the cliff, I wouldn't have just left him up there. From what he said last night at dinner, it sounded like he was excited about the Coast Guard—looking forward to going to Alaska. How could he go and kill Pete? Why would he mess up his life like that?"

Brie heard a mixture of fear and confusion in Will's voice. The kind she often heard when a young person was confronted with the ugliness of death. "I don't think there's a way to understand it, Will. It's not a rational act." She paused for a moment before pressing on. "Did anything else happen up there?"

"No. He just kept standing there with his back to me, so I headed back down the trail to the inn. I hadn't gone very far before I ran into Scott coming up the other way."

"Did you notice what time it was when you were up on the bluffs? It might help establish a time of death."

"I think it was around four o'clock, but I'm not sure of the exact time."

Brie sat for a moment deciding if she had any other questions. Will's recounting of Tim's agitated state was similar to what she'd seen up on the bluff. She stood up. "Can you think of any other details that might shed light on Tim's death?"

"I can't."

"That's all, then." Brie said. Will got up and they headed back down the hall to join the others.

Scott, George and Rob arrived back at the inn within forty-five minutes, loaded down with the equipment the captain had requested. They set everything down on the porch and came inside. Brie asked Howard if he would stay with Alyssa at the inn while the rest of them went up to retrieve the body. Howard happily agreed and immediately took Alyssa under his wing, asking her if she'd play a game of gin rummy with him. She was relieved to be left out of this harrowing task, and gladly settled in with Howard at the card table near the windows.

Out in the hall everyone donned their raincoats and headed for the porch to collect the equipment. There was a lot of gear, but with six people no one was overburdened. Coming back would be another story. They walked around the back of the inn toward the trail that led to the cliffs and were soon marching along single file into the woods.

15

DULAC LED THE PARTY OF SIX up the trail to recover the body. The rain was coming down hard again, making the footing quite slippery. Winding their way down the muddy trail carrying a body on a backboard with no handles would be some trick. They climbed through the spruce forest, finally stepping out onto the granite shelf where Tim was last seen alive. Piling the equipment on a slab of rock, they walked to the edge. Far below Tim's body bobbed up and down, still held prisoner by boulders near the base of the cliff.

"Let's get started," DuLac said. "We need to find the closest sturdy tree and tie off to it."

Scott walked back to the tree line. "There's one right here, Captain," he called.

"Good. You and George run a loop around the tree with the braided line and tie off to one of the blocks. Will and Rob, you rig up the long rope between the two blocks and tie one end to the bosun's sling."

Brie, Rob and Will got busy uncoiling the three hundred feet of rope and rigged it up as ordered.

When they were ready, Scott stripped down to his wet suit, rolled up his raincoat and foul-weather pants and stowed them out of the wind. He walked over to the edge of the cliff. They'd found a good spot to lower him that would put him near the inlet where the body was trapped. Scott climbed into the bosun's sling; John checked the knot on the sling and handed him the U-shaped rescue harness. He stationed Brie at the top of the cliff to call back directions, then walked back and formed a line on the rope with the other men.

"All set?" he called to Scott.

"Ready," Scott yelled. The men took up the slack, and Scott backed slowly over the edge.

They played out the rope, and when he was near the bottom, Brie called out, "Just a few more feet. Okay, stop, he's in the water."

Scott found his footing in the chest-deep water and climbed out of the sling. Pulling it behind him he swam toward Tim. The waves were breaking on a submerged rock ledge no more than fifteen feet beyond the body, and the tide was ebbing—both factors making Scott's job easier. Once he reached the body, he worked the rescue harness around Tim's back and under his arms. While doing so, he took in the damage caused by the fall. Tim's eyes were open, permanently fixed on the cloud deck sailing overhead. Long, thin fronds of sea wrack draped his body, their float bladders bobbing up and down as if they were keeping him suspended. His left leg splayed out at an unnatural angle below the knee, and the left side of his head was crushed. Even though Scott came from a medical family and had learned not to be squeamish, his stomach turned over at the sight. He worked as fast as he could in the frigid, chest-deep water, the cold already penetrating his wet suit. Balancing on the slippery rocks underfoot, he untied the rope from the sling and attached it to the harness. He turned and signaled Brie to lift away.

"Start hauling up," Brie called back to the men.

Slowly they brought up the body, the rescue harness holding it in a vertical position. When it was within three feet of the top, Brie called for them to stop. She went over to help on the rope and DuLac sent Rob and Will to maneuver the body over the edge of the cliff. They carried it back ten feet and laid it on the outspread tarp. Rob quickly untied the rope and brought it back over to the edge.

Scott had swum back to the foot of the cliff. Seeing the rope on its way down, he bobbed under water and pulled the bosun's sling between his legs. As they hoisted him up the wind swung him pendulum-like toward the wall, and he used his feet to repel off of it. As soon as he was safely on top, he climbed out of the sling and immediately headed for his pile of clothing. He shivered as he pulled on his foul-weather pants and raincoat, and then sat on the ground to put on his socks and hiking boots.

Brie was looking over the body, mentally cataloging the damage from the fall. When she got to his hands she paused. The skin on his right hand had been completely scraped off. Strange, she thought. It almost looked like he had grabbed for something on the way down. In that fateful moment, when he went over the edge, could he have changed his mind? Had he tried to grasp at something, tried to save himself, tried to call back his deadly decision? The only other possibility immediately registered in her detective's mind. He hadn't gone over voluntarily. But, thinking about Madie's death and the suicide note, she was inclined to dismiss this possibility.

Brie stood up and walked to the edge of the cliff where she'd last seen Tim alive. She looked over. Approximately ten and again twenty feet below the edge, a couple of rock ledges jutted out slightly. After that nothing but water and rocks far below. She walked back to the body, folded the tarp over it and taped it closed. The men were busy collecting the equipment and coiling the rope into a figure-eight-shaped pile. When they were finished, she called them over to lift the body onto the backboard. After they had tied it securely to the board, John and Rob took the front corners with Scott and Will at the rear. Between them George and Brie carried the heavy coil of rope and the rest of the equipment. The group disappeared into the pine forest, navigating slowly down the rain-soaked trail.

Glenn and Betty pulled up in front of the inn no more than fifteen minutes after the others had left. They walked in the front door and were surprised to be greeted by only Howard and Alyssa.

"Where are all the others?" Glenn asked.

"They're up on the bluffs," Howard said. "I'm afraid there's been another incident."

"What happened?" Betty asked, alarm ringing in her voice.

"Tim Pelletier, one of the passengers on the cruise, jumped off the cliff over there. Brie believes he murdered Pete and then committed suicide."

"Oh, my Lord!" Betty reached out for Glenn to steady herself. "We just met that young man this morning. He seemed so quiet and polite."

"The captain and the others have gone to retrieve his body," Howard continued. "I'm sorry, we didn't introduce ourselves. This is Alyssa Lindstrom and I'm Howard Thackeray."

Glenn and Betty shook hands with them. "Let's go in and sit down," Glenn said, motioning them into the game room, where they sat on the sofa and chairs surrounding the entertainment center.

"Does Brie know why he killed Pete?" Glenn asked.

"Apparently Tim blamed Pete for the death of his girlfriend. Brie said the girl died while on a rock climbing outing Pete was leading."

"Tim left a suicide note that Brie and Captain DuLac found when they discovered the body," Alyssa added. "It's all so horrible." She looked down at her hands, and her eyes filled with tears. Howard placed a comforting hand on top of hers.

"Poor John," Betty said. "He must be beside himself."

Glenn stood up. "I'm going to go clear out the back of the pickup truck. If they recover the body, John will need the truck to get down to the village."

"Can I help you?" Howard asked, eager for a manlier job.

"Sure," Glenn said. "I could use the help—it's full of tools."

"I'm going to prepare dinner for everyone," Betty said. "It's already late, and hopefully some warm food will be comforting."

"That's a great idea, dear. I'll be back in a few minutes and help you." Glenn and Howard put on their coats and headed out to bring the truck around to the garage.

"Why don't we go to the kitchen, and I'll make some tea," Betty said.

Alyssa brightened a little. "That'd be wonderful."

Out in the kitchen Betty put the kettle on the fire and got out a tray. She took down a china teapot with a delicate pink and gold design, along with matching cups and saucers. She could see how upset Alyssa was. "Are you on this cruise by yourself, dear?" she asked her.

"Oh, no, my husband Rob is with me. He went up with the others to help."

"Well, that's good," Betty said, relieved. Alyssa seemed fragile to her. Not physically—she appeared young and healthy—but on the inside, as if her well of inner strength might be running dry.

"Would you like to help me prepare the dinner after we have tea?" Betty asked her.

Alyssa jumped at the opportunity. "I'd love to. It will help take my mind off all of this."

Betty steeped the tea and set out a plate of iced lemon cookies. Alyssa helped her carry the things into the dining room, where they sat down together.

"Have you been married long, dear?" Betty asked.

"For five years. It seems longer, though," Alyssa said.

Betty sensed a loneliness in her. "Any children?" she asked.

"No, Rob doesn't want any—at least not yet. I'd like to, though."

"Well, I'm sure you will when the time is right," Betty said. "Do you work outside the home?"

"I work with Rob at his business. He owns a chain of photo finishing stores. I help with bookkeeping and office work." She stared at her tea cup.

Betty heard a profound lack of interest in Alyssa's voice.

"I'd like to have a gardening business." She glanced shyly up from her cup as if looking for Betty's approval.

"That sounds wonderful. Why don't you?"

"I wanted to go back to school—become a master gardener. I'd like to have a business of my own designing gardens for people." She took a cookie and started nibbling.

Betty could see that just talking about the idea provided an emotional transfusion. "Won't Rob support you in doing that?" she asked.

"He wants me to stay with the business. He wants me close by." Her voice fell. "He wants me to dress in skirts and high heels. He likes to show me off. And then he gets jealous when other people notice me. I hate it. At times I've wanted out so badly, I would have done anything." She looked at her half-eaten cookie, surprised she'd said these things to a stranger. There was something about Betty that made her feel safe. She wished she had someone like her back in Pittsfield to talk with. Someone motherly. There'd been no one like that in her life since her own mother had died eight years ago.

"I love the outdoors," she continued. "That's why I love to sail. Working outdoors—supervising the design and planting of gardens, and even doing some of the planting myself—I'd love that. It would be like a dream come true."

"Then you must share your dream with your husband. If he

really loves you, he'll support you in it," Betty said.

"Do you think so?"

"I do. In your mind's eye you need to see yourself accomplishing your dream. Then each day do something that moves you closer to that dream becoming a reality. Even if it's only for a half hour—do something toward it every day. That's how Glenn and I got here. It was our dream to retire to a place like this, and we worked hard at making it come true."

"Thank you, Betty," Alyssa said. She took another cookie and bit into it with gusto.

"You're very welcome, dear."

"I hope someone's lucky enough to have you for a mom."

Tears welled in Betty's eyes.

"Betty? What's wrong?"

Betty turned her head and stared out the window. "We did have a daughter," she said quietly. "She died in a car accident when she was seventeen." Betty bit down on her lip to stop the tears. "She'd have been about your age now."

"I'm so sorry." Alyssa took a small pack of tissues from her pocket and put one in Betty's hand.

"It's something you never get over. You just move on. It brought Glenn and me closer, and that's been a blessing. And buying this place has given us a focus." Betty dried her eyes and stood up, busying herself with the tea things. "It's been nice talking to you today, Alyssa."

"For me too, Betty."

"We should start on the dinner preparations. I'm thinking chicken and dumpling stew might be a good choice. What do you think?"

"I think the men will love that," Alyssa said, smiling. "And I bet you won't hear any complaints from Brie either."

"Good. Then let's get started." Alyssa picked up the tray and they headed into the kitchen.

"I like your cookies, Betty."

"I'll give you the recipe."

John and his crew moved slowly down the trail with the body. It was a painstaking process. In several places they had to tip the backboard on its side to get it through the trees. The slippery ground slowed their progress even more. At a brisk pace, the bluffs were about a fifteen-minute walk from the inn, but with the body in tow, it took them almost forty-five minutes. The rain had slacked to a heavy drizzle, but darkness was fast approaching, making visibility along the trail poor. Fog was cottoning the ground and as twilight fell, it looked like a forest filled with sleeping ghosts.

Glenn and Howard had emptied the truck. They were busy discussing the layout of Glenn's garage workshop, as well as their experiences in the Korean War, when they heard voices approaching. They walked out of the garage and saw John and the others just below the woods, approaching with the body. John was relieved to see Glenn there with the truck. They carried the body across the back lawn to the gravel driveway and slid the board into the truck bed. Scott headed for the inn to change into dry clothes.

"I suppose Howard has filled you in on our sad state of affairs," John said to Glenn.

"He has, and I'm sorry, John. Betty and Alyssa are cooking dinner. It's late and you must all be…" Glenn stopped abruptly, wondering if he should be talking about dinner over Tim's body.

"I think you'll find everyone's ready for a meal," John said as if reading his thoughts. "We'd planned to be out of your way and have dinner back on the ship. But I guess trying to plan anything on this trip is a risky proposition."

"It's okay, John. Betty and I will be happy to have everyone eat at the inn tonight. Are you heading down to the village right now?"

John nodded. "We're going to see if Fred has room for one more body in his cooler. Brie, why don't you hop in front with

George, and as soon as Scott's dressed we'll get going."

John talked to Glenn at the back of the truck while they waited, and in a few minutes Scott swung out the back door and jumped in the bed of the pickup truck for the ride down the hill. Gravel crunched under tires as they pulled down the driveway. John switched on the lights and turned left onto the dark road. The truck, bearing its grim cargo, disappeared around the bend.

16

THEY PARKED THE TRUCK IN FRONT of the general store. "All the lights are out," Brie said. "I think Fred's gone home."

"He doesn't have far to go—he lives upstairs above the store," John said. "There's a stairway around back. I'll go see if I can raise him."

John walked around the back of the store and up a double flight of open stairs, taking them two at a time. Outside the door there was a small balcony surrounded by a rickety wood railing. He opened the screen and knocked on the inside door. He heard footsteps and in a few moments the door opened, and Fred peered out.

"Captain DuLac," he said, opening the door a few more inches, his eyes wide with surprise. "Have you come to check on the body?"

John suppressed a smile. "I'm afraid it's more serious than that," he said, composing himself. "I'm afraid there's been another death."

"You don't say!" Fred opened the door all the way and looked around as if he half expected the body to be standing there. "Well, this is a serious turn of events." His last three words got the nod.

It was pretty serious after the first one, John thought to himself. "Would it be possible to make room for one more body in your cooler, Fred? It will only be till noon tomorrow. The Coast Guard should be here by then."

"Don't see why not," Fred chirped, as if he'd just been invited to a party. "I'll go get my keys. You wait right there, now, Captain," he admonished, as if John might change his mind and shop around for a better cooler.

Within a few seconds Fred popped out the door and led the way down the stairs.

"Let's go around front and get the others, Fred. They can help move things in the cooler."

When he saw them coming around the building, George opened the door. He and Brie got out, along with Scott, who vaulted over the side of the pickup. They walked up on the wooden porch and waited as Fred fumbled with the keys. He led the way through the door, flipping a light switch on the right-hand wall.

"Hello, again, Miss Beaumont," he said, turning eagerly to Brie. He nodded to Scott and George, but his eyes immediately returned to her. "I hear there's been another murder," he said, stretching his long neck toward her as if sharing a confidence.

"Actually, we believe it's a suicide, Fred."

"A suicide. You don't say. You don't say." His head moved back and forth as he processed this titillating bit of news. "Right here on the island. Imagine. Was it a gun? Did he shoot himself?"

"Actually, he jumped off the cliffs on the other side of the island and fell to his death." Brie decided to share the information, hoping it would keep Fred from doing his own investigation in the cooler after they left. She was pretty sure it was in the realm of possibility.

Fred led the way to the storeroom at the back, flipping on another light as they entered. He unlocked the heavy padlock hanging from the cooler and, pulling the door open, stuck his head in and turned on the light. Pete's body was against the right wall in its makeshift body bag, with food stacked along the other three walls. Fred craned his neck, giving directions as the others began moving crates of fruit and produce, eggs, milk, butter and cheese over to the left side of the cooler to make room for Tim's body along the back wall. Then they went back to the truck, slid the body out and carried it into the store as Fred held the door. Once the body was situated, they stepped out of the cooler, and after one last look, Fred relocked the door.

"Thanks so much, Fred," John said, shaking his hand. "You're a life saver." The irony of the phrase dawned on him as soon as it escaped his lips.

"Glad to be of help, Captain," Fred said gravely, momentarily straightening up to his full six-foot-three height.

"The Coast Guard will be here tomorrow, and you can get things back to normal," John said.

Fred visibly deflated. Brie felt a little sorry for him, knowing his moment of glory would be so short lived. They left by the front door and walked across the porch toward the truck. Below the hill the waters of the cove stretched out in front of them like black velvet.

"I'll sit back in the bed if you want, Scott," George said.

"Don't worry about it, George," Scott said, hoisting himself over the side of the pickup. Brie loved seeing men make that particular move—placing their hands on something chest high and simply vaulting over it. She had coined it the hormonal vault, the suddenness of it so captured the impulsive agility of young men.

John, Brie and George piled into the front seat and waved to Fred. He had paused on the porch, shoulders slightly hunched, one gangly arm raised in a goodbye—a stark contrast to Scott's athleticism. Poor Fred, Brie thought. He had been unlucky in what emerged from the gene pool, and she sensed it had led to a solitary and lonely life. Had he been in a more populated place, he might have found a mate, but here on the island his chances were slim. She inwardly wished him happiness.

John turned the truck around in the road and headed back out of town. It was a small pickup, and three adults across the front seat made for close quarters. As they bounced along the gravel road heading back up the hill to the inn, Brie was acutely aware of her body pressed against John's. She was also aware of a pleasant warmth that started in the pit of her stomach and traveled through her body. She remembered his playfulness in the library that afternoon and glanced over at him, trying to pick up a vibe. It immediately struck her that the only thing he was probably feeling right now was exhaustion. She hoped her closeness gave him a little comfort after this awful day.

It was 9:20 when they pulled up the driveway to the inn and parked in front of the garage. They headed down the flagstone path that led to the back door. Inside everyone was congregated in the kitchen waiting for them.

"Betty finished the dinner a little while ago," Glenn said, "but we wanted to wait until you four got back. Everything go all right?" he asked, studying John's face.

"Yup," John said, without elaborating. But Glenn could hear the tightness in his voice, and see it in his body—the laid-back ease with which he normally moved replaced by a kind of arthritis of anxiety.

"It smells wonderful, Betty," George said.

"Well, Alyssa gets half the credit," Betty said. "She helped with everything. Now, everyone carry the food into the dining room so we can get started."

Glenn picked up the stoneware tureen filled with chicken and dumpling stew, and Alyssa followed with a big bowl of mashed potatoes that smelled of butter and garlic. Will carried in a large bowl of salad, dressed with honey-mustard vinaigrette. Howard brought two wooden boards, each holding a loaf of crusty, piping-hot bread, and John, bringing up the rear, carried two carafes of coffee. Everyone gathered around the big table in the dining room, which sat twelve people—the total number of guests that the inn could accommodate. They passed the food around and started eating, and there was no shortage of grateful comments once everyone sampled Betty's cooking. Tense shoulders relaxed and stomachs were silenced as a powerful culinary contentment settled on the group.

"Betty, this is really delicious," John said. "Thank you."

"Alyssa, maybe Betty will give you her recipe," Rob suggested.

"She's certainly earned it," Betty said. "She helped me get this dinner together in record time."

"John, I'll come back to the ship with you and help you get the radio repaired," Glenn said. "If you're weighing anchor tomorrow, you'll need it fixed."

"Thanks, Glenn."

As they ate, Brie saw fatigue on the faces of her shipmates. After asking each of the passengers where they were from, Glenn and Betty let them eat quietly, and talked with John and Brie, who sat across the table from them.

"Glenn has been telling me about Ben and his lighthouse," Betty said. "Have you been out to visit him yet?"

"Not yet. I've been busy getting the *Maine Wind* ready for the season," John replied. "I've got a break in my cruise schedule in July and I'm planning to get out there then." He turned to Brie to explain. "Six months ago Ben inherited a lighthouse out on Sentinel Island. The light had been inactive for years, and the dwelling had fallen into total disrepair. His friend Harold McCann bought it from the lighthouse service for a song twenty-five years ago. Harold was a real recluse. He never married and had no close relatives. Ben was the only one who ever went out there to visit him. Harold left the place to him when he died, and now Ben plans to live out there in the summer. He'd always hoped to buy a place on an island one day."

"Sounds like a dream come true—having your own lighthouse," Brie said.

"That's what Ben thinks, too. He went out there at the end of April and has been busy painting and doing repairs."

"Is Ben married?" Brie asked.

"He's a widower—his wife died five years ago. This is the first thing I've seen him really excited about in years. I think it'll be good for him."

Within twenty minutes everyone had finished their dinner, and Betty served up strawberry rhubarb pie à la mode to go with the coffee. After dinner John sent Scott and George out to load all the equipment into the truck, while everyone else helped clean up from the meal. Glenn went upstairs to gather his tools and parts to repair the radio, and at 10:20, after thanking Betty and Glenn for their hospitality, everyone headed out to the truck. John told Brie and Alyssa to sit up front with Glenn, and he hopped in back with the other men for the drive down to the yawl boat.

17

GLENN PARKED THE TRUCK on the side of the road near where the yawl boat was tied up, and everyone piled out. Brie noticed Anna's lobsterboat still tied up where it had been earlier. There was a light on.

"I'll be right back, John," Brie said.

"Okay," he said over his shoulder as they began unloading the gear.

Brie walked down to the dock and stopped next to Anna's boat. "Ahoy," she called. Anna stepped up out of the cabin, looking surprised. She smiled when she saw it was Brie.

"Hey," she said.

"I saw the light in your wheel house and just wanted to make sure everything was all right," Brie said.

"Thanks, Brie—that's really nice. I'm just splicing some line and having a cup of coffee. I like it down here at night. It's so peaceful."

Brie understood Anna's connection to her boat and her work.

She'd certainly lived for her own work for enough years.

"How's the investigation going?" Anna asked.

"It's coming along." Brie didn't want to get into the details of Tim's death with Anna because she knew John was waiting to head back to the ship.

"If you aren't busy in the morning, why don't you come out with me for a couple hours and haul some traps—have an authentic Maine experience? You can tell your friends about it back in Minneapolis," she said.

"The Coast Guard is coming around noon. Would we be back in time?" Brie asked.

"Plenty of time. I'll have you back by 11:00. You'll have to get up early though, if you don't mind."

"I've always been an early riser," Brie said. "I'd love to come."

"Great," said Anna. "Then I'll pick you up about 6:30."

"I'm looking forward to it." Brie walked off the dock and back to where her shipmates were boarding the yawl boat.

They headed across the harbor toward the *Maine Wind*. The gale had finally blown itself out. Stars were beginning to show through the last remnants of the storm's cloud deck, and overhead fast-moving ghosts sailed across the moon. Brie looked toward the *Maine Wind*. One more chapter had just been added to the schooner's rich history. She thought about all the storms the fine old ship had weathered and felt a sudden affinity for her. Going back to the *Maine Wind* tonight felt like going home.

After all the passengers were unloaded, Scott and George got the equipment off the yawl boat, brought it down to the storeroom and carried up four kerosene lanterns. John went below to his cabin with Glenn to get started on the radio repair. Rob, Alyssa, Will and Howard said they were turning in and headed below to their cabins. Brie went to change her muddy jeans, then headed for Tim's cabin to look for a handwriting sample.

After helping George light and distribute the lanterns, Scott went below to see what the captain had planned for the watch.

"I'll take the first watch," DuLac said. "You come on deck and relieve me at 0200, and George can take the watch from 0500 to 0700."

"Sounds good. I'm turning in then, if it's okay?" Scott said.

"Go ahead," John nodded. "I'm heading up on deck in a couple minutes. Glenn's the expert here—he doesn't need my help making these repairs."

"See you at 0200 then, Captain." Scott climbed the companionway ladder and headed for his bunk at the other end of the ship.

Brie snapped on the reading light in Tim's cabin and began going through his belongings. She didn't remember having seen a journal or notebook when she was in here the first time, but searched through everything anyway. They'd retrieved Tim's wallet from his pocket after they brought him up, but it was of no help, the contents having been in the salt water long enough to dissolve any writing. Her search of the cabin came up empty. She was about to leave when she thought about the picture of him and Madie. She opened the back of the frame and extracted the photo. Sure enough, there was handwriting on the back—an almost illegible scrawl that she finally deciphered. It read: *Tim and Madie: Camping and climbing weekend in Acadia National Park.* If this was Tim's writing, Brie wasn't surprised that he'd printed the suicide note. It had obviously been important to him to convey his motivation. She pulled the note out of her pocket to compare the two writing samples. The note had been carefully printed and seemed to bear no relationship to the writing on the picture.

She decided to ask both Will and Scott for samples of their handwriting since they had both been gone from the inn for awhile, and the exact time of Tim's death was not known. As she left Tim's cabin, Will appeared carrying a basin of wash water. He headed up on deck to discard it, and when he came back down, she asked him to step into Tim's cabin and give her a handwriting sample.

"What do you need that for? You said it was a suicide." He tried to keep his anger at bay, but it had already infiltrated his voice.

"It's just part of following procedure until we can obtain a sample of Tim's handwriting and verify that it matches the suicide note. I'll be asking Scott for one, too."

"But what possible motive could I have for killing Tim?" Will pursued, as if he hadn't heard a word she'd said.

"None that I can think of offhand, so I guess you needn't worry." She was tired and his tone irritated her.

"And if I were going to kill him, do you think I'd leave a note in my own handwriting? Do I look stupid?"

"I don't know, Will. Do you?" she asked, deciding that he actually bore a slight resemblance to a pit bull. She wondered if they were stupid.

Grudgingly, Will provided a sample of both his printing and his handwriting. Brie could see, even without comparing them, that they were distinctly different from the note, but she was glad she'd checked it out.

George had gone down to the galley to stoke up Old Faithful and make coffee for the watch. Brie stuck her head down the companionway.

"George, have you seen Scott?" she asked.

"He turned in a little while ago. Do you want me to get him?"

"No. I'll catch up with him tomorrow."

"You sure?"

"Yup. Mind if I join you for a while?"

"I'd love some company, Brie. C'mon down. It'll be warmer in a few minutes once the stove gets going." He set out coffee beans and a coffee mill with a crank on the top. "Would you like to grind the coffee?"

"Sure," said Brie. "How much should I do?"

"Why don't you grind up three quarters of a cup of beans—that'll make twelve cups of coffee, which should get us through the night." While Brie ground the beans, George finished feeding the stove and put on the water for the coffee.

"So how did you ever end up cooking on a windjammer?" she asked as she turned the crank on the coffee grinder.

"My family's from New York City," George began. "They run a Greek deli down there. Have for three generations now." His olive skin and dark eyes glowed in the yellow light from the lantern. He had pushed up the sleeves of his sweatshirt, and the black curly hair on his arms exactly matched the stuff on top of his head. "I first saw the big ships when I was a boy. We had come up to Maine on a vacation—all eight of us in an old station wagon. We used to fight over the back seat that faced out toward the road. I guess there was something exciting about seeing where you'd been, and from back there you could make faces at the driver behind you, and your dad never knew."

Brie laughed, remembering the back seat of her family's Oldsmobile—how she'd vied with her brothers for the seat by the window. Mom and Dad were never conscientious enough about the fair distribution of window-seat time. And being stuck between those two, with that big hump under her feet, had been a terrible fate. Her thoughts slid back to tonight's ride up from the village in Glenn's truck and the feel of John's body next to hers.

"How are the beans comin'?"

"They're comin'."

George continued. "We rented a house near Rockport and took day trips up and down the coast. We rode ferries out to islands and had picnics in a different spot every day. And every-where we went there were sailboats, shooshing along silently with their starched, white sails." His arms gestured gracefully. "Some-times we were close enough to hear laughter, or orders being shouted; the slap of halyards against the masts, or the creak of rigging when they'd come about. I fell in love with the whole idea. And while my brothers and sisters seemed content enough in the city helping with the family business, I had a different vision. As

169

for cooking, well, I was born to that. In our family, food anchors every occasion. In high school I was good at two things. The shot-put and cooking classes.

"So, seven years ago, when I was 23, I came to Maine to see if I could get a job on one of the windjammers. I'd never sailed a day in my life, and Captain DuLac was the only one who seemed interested in me, but he had a cook. He said he'd keep my name, though, and two years later I got a call from him asking me if I was still interested. He said he'd give me a try if I could come to Maine and sail with him and the crew for a couple weeks—see how I took to the ship and how I cooked. That was five years ago, and, well, here I still am. During the off season I go back to the city and help my older brother. He opened a small restaurant in midtown Manhattan two years ago, and I'm always welcome in the kitchen there." He smiled. "I'll admit I'm not getting rich, but I'm happy. And I wouldn't trade my time on the *Maine Wind* for anything."

The water was boiling. George took the coffee grounds from Brie and put them in the basket of his big drip pot that sat on the stove. Then he poured the hot water into the basket, adding more as it dripped through. Once the coffee reached the twelve-cup level, he transferred it into the two carafes to keep it hot.

"So, what's for breakfast tomorrow, George? I'm going out on a lobsterboat in the morning to have an 'authentic Maine experience.' Just wondering what I'll be missing."

"Actually, I'm making egg noodles."

"*Reeeally,* trying to tempt me, eh? I don't know, George, I'm pretty set on going lobstering."

"Well, in that case I'm making cinnamon French toast with bacon on the side. Is that enough to keep you aboard?"

Brie smiled at him, feeling the responsibilities of the last hours lifting a little. "You sure make it hard on a girl. You know it's not often a Midwesterner has a chance to help haul lobster traps. So, much as I love French toast, I guess I'll have to pass."

"Maybe not. What time are you leaving?"

"Six-thirty sharp."

"That early, eh? Guess I can't whip anything up for you, then, since I have the watch from 0500 to 0700. Tell you what, though, I always stoke the stove by 0500, so I'll make some coffee before I go on watch. Why don't you come down to the galley before you leave and scramble yourself a couple of eggs? You'll need your strength if you're going to work stern tomorrow."

"That'd be great, but I don't want you getting up early on my account."

"It'll only take me ten minutes, Brie. I don't mind."

"Well, okay then. I'll come down to the galley by six."

He ran a hand through his thick hair. "I'd better turn in now, or I'm gonna regret it tomorrow."

"See you in the morning, George."

"Night, Brie."

18

BRIE CLIMBED UP THE LADDER and started aft. There was a chill in the air, but the sky had totally cleared, and what a sight it was. Thousands of stars of varying magnitudes filled the night sky. She smiled, remembering her college astronomy. To the south, the Milky Way stretched out, creaming its way toward the center of the galaxy some 35,000 light years away. Brie just stood there in awe as she always did at this sight. A few moments later she heard voices, and John and Glenn emerged from the aft companionway. She walked toward them.

"Brie. I thought you'd turned in," John said.

She thought she detected a note of quiet delight in his voice at her still being up. "I was talking to George down in the galley while he made coffee. How'd it go with the radio, Glenn?"

"Good as new. You should be all set to sail back to the mainland tomorrow. It certainly has been a pleasure getting to know you, Brie."

"I feel the same way. And Glenn, thank you for letting us use the inn today. It made everyone's day a lot easier. I'm just sorry about the circumstances."

"Those were beyond your control, Brie. You're always welcome at Snug Harbor." Glenn put a hand on John's shoulder. "You remember what I told you, son."

"Yes, sir," John said, glancing briefly over his shoulder at Brie. He climbed over the stern, took the box that Glenn handed him and made his way down the ladder to the yawl boat. Glenn went next. John helped him into the boat and then called back up to Brie, "I'll be back in a little while. If you wouldn't mind waiting up, I'd like to talk to you."

"No problem," Brie said.

John gave her a two-finger salute, started up the yawl boat and pulled away.

Brie leaned against the rail and looked across the water toward the horizon line where sea and stars met. There, hung in the southern sky, were Deneb, Altair and Vega, old friends she'd met years ago when she studied astronomy—when she'd discovered where she really stood in the grand scheme of things. Oddly enough, learning about the size of the universe had never made her feel insignificant. Quite the opposite, in fact. She felt at one with something grand and mysterious—a student of arcane knowledge, knowledge that could, at once, let her glimpse the boundaries of the universe or the borderless expanses of the mind. Standing as she was, on the deck of spaceship Earth, she thought about time and infinity and chance encounters between people. Were they chance? Or did the same force that sent the stars, planets, and galaxies reeling in motion about one another, draw people into each other's orbits as well, setting them on intersecting pathways. Was there a profound plan at work weaving together strands of tragedy, love, loss and hope to form a bridge over unimaginable chasms?

The yawl boat was surprisingly close when Brie finally heard it, so lost was she in her reverie. Moments later, John climbed over the stern of the ship and walked toward her.

"Hey," she said.

"Hey, yourself," he replied. The amber light from the lantern fell across her face as he approached, and for just a moment, he paused, feeling a strange yet familiar tug as if something were both far away and very near.

"What is it?" Brie asked, seeing his expression.

"Nothing, just...just a funny feeling; something familiar but fleeting, and you don't know why. Does that ever happen to you?"

She studied his eyes, remembering the moment they'd met and the silence that had fallen on her heart, like the stopping of time. "Sometimes," she said, looking back toward the sea.

John leaned against the rail. He couldn't believe it was just yesterday they'd stood in this same place talking about Lake Superior, not really knowing each other at all. Tonight, he felt like he'd known her forever. "You look like you're a million miles away again."

"I've been dancing along the Milky Way."

"Sounds romantic. Can I join you?"

"It's not for the faint of heart," she said, looking at him.

"Neither is sailing a windjammer." He reached out as he spoke, picking up a strand of her long silky hair and sliding it through his fingers. "So, tell me, what is Brie short for?"

"It's short for Briana," she said, a slight quaver in her voice.

"Briana Beaumont. That's a rather lyrical name for a police detective."

"Actually, it's a good one," she said. "Did you know that Briana is from the Celtic, meaning strength and honor?"

"It suits you well then." He fell silent for a moment.

"Something the matter, John?"

"I can't help thinking about Pete. Or Tim, for that matter."

An errant wave slapped against *Maine Wind's* hull.

"I know," she said. "It'll take a while before that goes away. Sudden, violent death is shocking and disturbing, so the mind keeps revisiting it."

"Tim certainly didn't strike me as a killer."

"Even the gentlest dog will bite if provoked enough. Without too much effort we can all picture a situation in which we would kill another. What we call motive or motivation is often nothing more than justification, and in the human mind, that can be a very subjective thing." She waved a hand. "Sorry, I'm preaching."

"No, Brie. Go on."

"Well, in order to kill, the average person would have to be put in a situation where his life or the life of a loved one was threatened. But grief does strange things to the mind—twists it in strange ways."

Brie scanned the stars overhead. "I was picking out star constellations. Do you know most of them?" she asked, hoping to get his mind off the deaths.

"I used to. Ben taught me to navigate by the stars. He was a career navy man and a master of celestial navigation."

Brie had been assembling a mental picture of John's mentor for the past couple of days, and this was one more interesting bit of information to help flesh out that picture.

John continued. "Ben used to make me pick out the constellations when we were out on the ocean at night." He extended his arm. "There's Hercules, directly overhead. And below it, Boötes —The Herdsman." He stopped and looked down at his hands on the rail. "Ben always took the time to teach me things—to explain things. He wasn't my dad but in certain ways…"

"He was more of a dad than your real one?" Brie looked at him shyly, wondering if she'd overstepped her bounds.

"Yes," he said quietly. "I've never been able to admit that—till now. I guess I wanted to hold onto this glorified image of my dad—maybe because he died when I was so young. But that image has caused me a lot of anger over the years." John pointed to a very bright star in the west. "Do you know the name of that one?"

"That's Arcturus. It's the fourth brightest star in the sky—

only thirty-four light years away. In space that's like your next-door neighbor."

"You know something about all this, don't you?"

Brie smiled. "A little."

"There's Scorpius," John said, pointing out the constellation. "The stars at the end look just like a scorpion's tail."

"That bright star just above the middle is Antares. Now that's a big star," Brie said. "A red supergiant—it's huge compared with our sun, and a long way off. I think around 600 light years."

"It *looks* red. What causes that?"

"It's an old star, and it doesn't burn as hot as the young ones. The light Antares sends out is a longer wavelength, and so it appears red. The hottest stars appear blue—they send out a much shorter wavelength of light."

John smiled, seeing her passion for this. "So—any young stars out tonight?"

Brie pointed toward the zenith. "See the Northern Cross? The star at the tip of the cross is Deneb—a blue-white supergiant. It's younger and much hotter than Antares."

John fixed her with a smoldering gaze. "So are you."

Brie smiled, but her throat had gone tight like she might have just lost her ability for speech.

John stepped closer. "Don't stop. I like hearing about this." He ran a finger along her jaw. "Tell me about these light years."

Light years, Brie thought. Who cares about light years? She glanced at him, wondering why he had to be so darn handsome. It was unnerving.

"As I recall, a light year is a whole lot of time," John prompted.

Brie was hoping they'd wrap up this discussion soon and move on to something completely nonverbal. "Well," she said, "light moves at 186,000 miles per second. That's about eleven million miles in just one minute. So try to imagine how far it goes in a year. Space is a big place—like I said, not for the faint of heart." A soft breeze lifted her hair, and it glowed gold in the lantern light.

"So what is it about the stars, Brie? What *really* intrigues you?"

Brie looked at him, surprised by his seeming ability to see into her. "I guess they're a lot like people. Knowable but unknowable. I mean we can chart them, classify them, analyze their light spectrums to see what they're made of. But in another way we know nothing, because the light from most stars started traveling so long ago. In space you never see things as they really are, only as they were." She looked at John earnestly. "But mostly I'm just fascinated by what's out there. Studying it...well, it changed the way I think about pretty much everything. It made me think big. I guess you could say I was altered by astronomy."

"You know what?" John said, holding her eyes. "I like the results."

The coolness of the night was working on Brie. She shivered. "It's starting to get cold," she said. "I think I'll go grab my jacket."

"I have a better idea," John said, catching her hand as she started to walk away. He pulled her over and, circling his arms around her waist, stepped behind her, pressing his body against hers for warmth. They stood at the rail looking out to sea. John felt another shiver run through her and wondered if she could sense his desire, which he just barely had in check. Being a detective, she probably could. He was still bothered by that phone call from Garrett and wondered what Brie's relationship with him was—and what it had been. He sure seemed territorial about her. Oh, damn Garrett, he thought. I have the advantage—I'm here, she's here, I'm the captain of this great old schooner, I'm not bad looking...

Brie leaned back into him, a bundle of sensations. Feelings of safety and desire ran through her like a warm current. There was refuge in his strong arms and there was passion in those molten brown eyes of his. She liked John's easy-going manner, but she also liked the captain in him. The past few days, she'd seen him take control of several difficult situations. And there was a physical presence about him she'd witnessed in other men who pitted themselves against the elements. *Just face it, Brie, he's a hunk. But one you have no future with. Tomorrow you'll be heading back to the mainland, and he'll be heading back out to sea for the rest of the summer.*

As if reading her thoughts, John turned her around to face him. "What would you think about staying on the *Maine Wind* this summer?" he asked. "I'll be needing a second mate, and with your sailing background you've got all the right qualifications."

Brie was thinking about being a mate all right, just not the kind that climbs masts for a living. But the possibility intrigued her. She wasn't ready to go back to Minneapolis—that much she did know. Staying aboard the *Maine Wind*, though, with John? That could lead to something that wouldn't be so easy to resolve.

"Um, I'm not sure," she said, looking up into his eyes. "I hadn't decided how much longer I was staying in Maine. I guess I'd like to think about it."

"That's fine," John said, still holding her captive in his arms. He brushed aside a lock of hair as it blew across her face. "Maybe this will help you decide." Leaning down, he kissed her lips gently, lingering there, letting her just taste him. Brie's arms involuntarily went around his neck, and John, drawing her close, kissed her like the sun might never rise again on planet Earth.

In every woman's life there are a few unforgettable kisses. For Brie there'd been just two others, and they finished first and second runners-up to this one. John relaxed his hold on her, and she swayed, light-headed. She decided that she definitely hadn't done enough kissing lately. She wondered if she was free to move, or if the rubber soles of her sneakers had melded to the deck. When she looked up at John, he was slightly out of focus. He seemed to be smiling—probably the smug look of any man that can kiss like that, she thought. But then his face swam back into focus, and she realized that it wasn't smugness. He was just looking kind of daffy—a sign that her return kiss was not without impact.

John leaned toward her again, but Brie put a hand on his chest, gently stopping him. "You wouldn't want my decision to be biased by undue sexual influence, would you?"

"I might if it helps you say 'yes' to my offer."

"If I stay aboard, we'll have to maintain a working relationship—i.e. you're the captain and I'm part of the crew."

"Does that mean I can order up a kiss whenever I want?" He nuzzled the side of her head, kissing the top of her ear.

"Very funny, and no it doesn't," Brie said, trying, but not very hard, to wiggle out of his arms. She was having a monumental inner struggle keeping her distance. And she was really glad they were up on deck and not below near either of their cabins, since she'd already fantasized plenty about rolling around in one of those snug little berths with him.

"Seriously, John, I couldn't function as part of the crew if we were romantically involved. I have to be okay with you barking out orders, and what if we were having a bad day—an argument, say—it could affect my performance on the ship."

"You mean to tell me you've never had a relationship with anyone you've worked with?"

"That's right, I haven't. At home, in the police department, I wouldn't even entertain the thought."

So much for Garrett, John thought smugly.

"You crewed for your dad. Weren't you ever having a bad day with him?"

"That's different, and you know it, but yes, occasionally I was, and it did make it harder. And there it was just our family aboard —there weren't any passengers involved."

"But..." he took a step toward her, his expression halfway between helpless and desperate. "But what about this?" He waved a hand between them. "You kissed me back—that means you're interested too."

Brie sighed and stepped into him, laying her head on his chest. "I am interested, John. And I'm more than a little attracted to you. But my career is back in Minnesota, 1500 miles away, and if I stay here for the summer, it could make the decision about whether or not to go back even harder. And if we got involved—what would that make the decision?"

"I don't know, Brie, maybe it would make it easier," he said matter-of-factly.

 Brie looked at him like they were speaking two different languages. "Let me sleep on it, John," she said. "I promise I'll let you know before we get back to port. Oh, and I almost forgot to tell you, I'm going out on a lobsterboat in the morning with a woman I met in the village. She has her own boat. She thought I might like to come out with her and see what lobstering's all about."

"But the Coast Guard is supposed to be here by noon."

"I know, and she promised to have me back by 11:00."

"Well, okay, but you be careful out there. Even though the gale has passed, the seas will still be running high. I wouldn't want to lose my potential second mate."

"I'll be careful, John. Remember, I cut my sailing teeth on Lake Superior. But I need to turn in now."

He lifted her chin up and kissed her lips gently, and his presence, coupled with the salt air, was so intoxicating that, for just a moment, she had a longing to stay with him on the deck of this ship forever. She forced herself to take a step away from him.

"Goodnight, John," she said, softly. She walked past him toward the companionway, not noticing the shadow that moved across the dimly lit deck up near the bow.

"Goodnight, sweet Brie," he said, just as she reached the top of the ladder.

Brie froze in her tracks. No one in her life, except her dad, had ever used that expression. It was what he'd said to her every night of her young life. *Goodnight, sweet Brie, sweet dreams.* She looked at John curiously, and a palpable energy passed between them. Shaken, she disappeared down the ladder. She'd always been a firm believer in signs, but this one had really unsettled her, and she badly wanted to dismiss it as coincidence.

She bolted into her cabin, shutting the door, and grabbed her wash basin to tap off some cold water. She needed that coldness on her face—needed it to bring her back to reality. She lingered over the bowl, splashing water against her skin. What was he doing using that phrase? She felt as if he'd looked into her psyche and picked the one thing that could most influence her. What really scared her, though, was that it had placed an immediate and inescapable warmth around her heart. "This isn't happening," she said as she stripped off her jeans and pulled on her leggings. "This can't be happening—not here, not now." Over the past five years she'd made several attempts at relationships, but they'd all fizzled—some sooner, some later. And none of them, not even the one that lasted over a year, had had a flicker of the intensity that passed between her and John when they merely looked at each other.

Brie got into her bag, pulled it up to her chin and lay there for some time, thinking about her life back home. Over the past twelve years of relentless dedication to her work, she'd piled up a very comfortable amount of savings, as well as tons of vacation time. But lying here now, she had to admit to herself that she hadn't stored up much happiness. And, for the first time, the realization of how alone she was poured like a flood tide into her consciousness. Her friends had, one by one, married and started families, while she hadn't even managed to find Mr. Right. Her mother had remarried two years ago and moved to the southwest, and her brothers had their own families. But, worst of all, since the shooting of her partner last year, she had felt alienated from her work—the one thing that had meant the most to her. She realized she was more alone than she'd ever been in her life.

What was more, over the past couple of days the little voice inside her head had been getting louder in its insistence that maybe there wasn't that much to go home to. *Move to Maine, though—even if it is just for the summer? That would mean jeopardizing everything I've worked so hard for. That's crazy, isn't it?* But a pleasant sensation of heaviness, coupled with a feeling of floating, was taking over her being, as if she were a hot air balloon tethered in place. "It's crazy, isn't it?" she murmured. One last image crossed her mind before her balloon took flight; it was of a pair of warm brown eyes followed by two simple words—*home port*.

Above where Brie slept, John walked the deck uneasily. Not since his father died had he felt such a complete lack of control over his own life, and he knew what he desperately longed for could slip like sand through his fingers. He went below to the galley to pour himself a mug of coffee. Once back on deck he walked aft and sat down on a wooden storage locker. Leaning back against the rail, he stretched out his long legs and thought about how much he wanted Brie with him this summer—how much he wanted her.

The ship had swung at anchor and now faced into a steady, but much gentler westerly wind. John realized his life had also swung to a different bearing. He felt temporarily adrift—at the mercy of elements well beyond his control—uncertain of what lay ahead or which way the winds would blow. And while the captain in him was used to this feeling, even excited by it, the man in him wasn't so sure.

He got up and took another turn around the deck. He'd always liked the solitude of the watch, but tonight it was oppressive. He felt restless and alone. He stopped at the rail and looked across the ink-dark water. Blackness shrouded the harbor and the village beyond, where the bodies of two men lay—the secret of what had really happened on deck that night as still and silent as they. John shivered, an odd feeling passing over him. Something seemed wrong. But how could it not? Two men had died. He wrote his feeling off to extreme fatigue and checked his watch. Still another hour till Scott took over. He walked silently aft under the stars.

19

BRIE WOKE TO A CRYSTALLINE DAWN whose clarity was equaled only by that in her own mind. Like the ball on a roulette wheel, her decision, at least for the near future, had dropped into a specific slot, and she hoped it held her lucky number. She resisted questioning the decision, knowing that when you wake with that kind of certainty, it's a gift.

She hopped up and, grabbing her towel, soap and shampoo, headed for what qualified as a shower at the end of the passageway. She was back in her cabin in ten minutes and slicked her damp hair back into a ponytail. She pulled on a pair of washed-out jeans, a heavy cotton sweater and her canvas deck shoes. She loaded a fresh roll of film into her camera and grabbed her rain slicker, deciding it was the best option for keeping her clothes dry while they hauled traps. She realized she was excited about going out with Anna today, and noted that it was the first time in quite a while she'd felt that way. Maybe her lucky number had come up.

Brie headed up on deck, planning to hit the galley and scramble a couple of eggs, as George had encouraged. Emerging from the companionway, she saw him sitting on the forward cabin top, drinking a mug of coffee. She hailed him.

"Hey, George, what a morning!"

"Sure is. Maybe this trip will at least end on a good note."

"Let's hope so," she said, stopping in front of him. "That stove going?"

"I kept my word. The eggs are waiting and there's hot coffee."

"George, you're the best."

"There's a skillet down there with the butter already in it—all you have to do is scramble the eggs."

"Can I make a couple for you while I'm at it?"

"No thanks. I can never face food this early in the morning. I can cook it, just can't eat it."

Brie headed below and set the skillet on the burner. Within a minute the butter started to sizzle, and she cracked in the eggs, stirring them around. She sliced off a thick piece of bread from the loaf George had set out and spread it with apricot preserves. Scrambling the eggs around a little more, she slid them onto a plate. Then, filling her mug with coffee, she climbed back up on deck to eat her breakfast with him. They sat together silently, enjoying the peace of the early morning light on the sea. Brie noticed the wind had shifted into the west, promising good sailing back to the mainland.

At 6:25 the quiet was interrupted by the sound of a motor starting up at one of the docks.

"That must be your ride," George said.

Brie hurried below and washed off the plate, mug and skillet she'd used. When she came back up, a lobsterboat was cutting slowly across the harbor toward the *Maine Wind*. Just then Brie saw John emerge from the aft companionway and head forward.

"Hey Skipper," George called. "You're supposed to be asleep for another half hour."

"I know, but I wanted to see Brie off."

George noted the look that passed between them and wondered just what had gone on last night after he'd hit the sack.

Anna idled her motor as she approached the stern of the *Maine Wind* and drifted slowly up to the ship. Brie and John walked aft, and George noted the captain's arm around her waist. Something's developing, he thought, and it couldn't happen to two nicer people. George knew that he, Scott and the captain all shared a common thread of independence, but he was also aware that the captain had seemed less settled the last couple of seasons. George had decided he needed something, and it wasn't too hard to figure out what that was. He thought Brie fit the bill nicely.

John caught Brie's arm as she started to climb over the stern. "Remember what I said last night, Brie. Be careful."

"I'm a sailor, John. We're careful by nature. See you in a few hours," she said, climbing down the ladder.

When she jumped onto the deck of the *Just Jake*, Anna turned and hailed her.

"Hi, Brie. Welcome aboard."

"Anna, meet Captain DuLac." She raised a hand toward John, who was looking over the stern of the *Maine Wind*. "John, this is Anna Stevens."

"Hi, Anna. Great morning, isn't it."

"Sure is," she yelled over the steady rumble of her boat's engine. "You weighing anchor today?"

"We're hoping to," John called back. He left it at that, not knowing what Brie had told her about the Coast Guard's arrival.

"C'mon forward, Brie," Anna said. "I'll let you drive."

Brie waved to John before stepping into the wheel house. After a few instructions from Anna, she took the wheel and motored clear of the *Maine Wind*. Then, as John watched, they took off out of the cove and headed north, up the western side of the island.

The wind was kicking up a little. *Just Jake* cut smoothly across the water, sending out a large enough wake to counteract a rather laid-back incoming surf. Gulls were circling and calling, excited about the fishing possibilities this sun-washed morning presented.

"I thought we'd head up this way—give you a chance to see the top of the island. I've got one group of traps up here, but most of mine are on the other side of the island." As she spoke Anna poured out a cup of coffee and handed it to Brie.

"Thanks. I could use a little more coffee. Hope this is the same stuff you had the other day."

"The very same," Anna said, smiling.

Brie handed the wheel over to Anna so she could drink her coffee and enjoy the view of the island. They were starting to see lots of brightly colored buoys now as the water near the island became shallower.

"How deep are these traps set?" Brie asked.

"This time of year most are set in 10 to 15 fathoms."

Brie did the math in her head—60 to 90 feet deep. "Who decides on the buoy colors?" she asked.

"They're assigned by the state and printed on your Maine State Lobster License. My colors are green, red, yellow."

"So you work alone?" Brie asked.

"At this time of year it's pretty slow. When school gets out, I'll have a sixteen-year-old kid working stern for the summer." Anna switched topics. "Say, a couple of people noticed the goings on at Fred's store last night. What's this about another body?"

Brie wished she didn't have to talk about bodies on this beautiful morning, but didn't want to appear rude, either.

"The case is shaping up to look like a murder-suicide. Apparently Tim—one of the passengers—killed Pete and then jumped to his death over on the east side of the island. Before it becomes official, though, I need to get another sample of his handwriting to compare to the suicide note we found. That will have to wait till we get back to the mainland."

"So you're just waiting for the Coast Guard?"

"That's right. As soon as they get here to collect the bodies, we're weighing anchor."

"Well, I hope it goes smoothly," Anna said with sincerity. She pointed off to starboard. "There's my first bunch of buoys."

While they'd been talking, Brie saw by the compass that they were veering east, traveling along the northern shore of the island. Slowing the boat to a crawl, Anna started weaving through dozens of brightly colored buoys toward the ones she'd pointed out. They had glo-green tops with stripes of crimson red and a screaming shade of yellow.

"Now we go to work," Anna said. "I'm going to circle up next to a buoy, Brie. You take the gaff that's over on the starboard rail and hook the buoy. I'll be right there."

Brie followed directions, and as Anna slowly circled the boat in, moving barely above an idle, Brie hooked the first buoy. Anna was at her side in a moment. She reached over the gunwale and grabbed the line attached to the bottom of the buoy. "This line is called pot warp, Brie. There are two traps on each line." She fed it through a block and into a hydraulic hauler which, when activated, pulled the traps up. Slowly the line accumulated on the deck, and, eventually the first trap broke the surface of the water. Anna reached over and brought it up on the rail. She told Brie to pull the second trap on the line—called the trailer—which broke the surface a few moments later. The traps each contained three bricks to hold them in place on the ocean floor, and they were surprisingly heavy, even empty. Brie suddenly realized the strength and endurance this job would require and had to admire the ease with which Anna pulled the 3-foot-long traps up onto the gunwale of the boat, time and again.

"How many of these do you haul in a day?" Brie asked.

"Usually about two hundred if I have a sternman—fewer if I'm working alone."

"Wow!"

"You earn your money the hard way in this job."

"Hopefully you catch more than we are today." They had been

working their way along the shore for quite a while and had pulled several dozen traps. So far they had gleaned only nine keepers, which Anna had banded and tossed into a box on the deck.

"This is usually the slow part of the season. It'll pick up as summer wears on," she said with surprising confidence.

Brie decided she'd never be able to gamble her income on the comings and goings of a bunch of creepy crawlers captured through backbreaking labor. She felt renewed gratitude for the education her parents had provided for her.

"Break time," Anna announced after they'd finished the next five buoys.

Brie checked her watch and was surprised to find they'd already been gone for almost two and a half hours.

Stepping back to the wheel, Anna maneuvered the boat clear of the forest of buoys, motored out a ways from shore and cut the engine. She slipped the wide suspenders off her shoulders and stepped out of her oilskins that she wore when working. Then she grabbed the thermos of coffee, a jug of water, and a brown paper bag that contained an assortment of candy bars. "Let's go aft," she said. "We can sit on the storage locker." It was a near perfect morning—the breeze was cool but the sun warmed them.

"I make myself take a break every couple hours, or I'd never get through the day," Anna said.

"I can believe that," Brie said. She took off her raincoat and laid it on the deck.

They were about to sit down when Anna noticed something was sticking out of the locker. She lifted the lid to tuck it back in. Brie saw a couple of spare buoys and floats, as well as some scuba and snorkel gear. "Are you a diver?" she asked, seeing yet another side to Anna.

"Yup," Anna said, closing the locker without further comment and sitting down on top of it. She stretched her long, denim-clad legs out in front of her, pulled her arms above her head and arched backwards over the gunwale. "I call this the reverse curl," she said lightly. "It makes up for all the bending over. Give it a try, Brie."

Brie took in Anna's long, lean body. She'd noticed that Anna was tall when she'd interviewed her yesterday, but somehow, she was more aware of her height today. Maybe because she wasn't wearing baggy rain gear, or maybe because her height coupled with her athletic strength was impressive.

"My dad taught me to dive," she said, returning to Brie's question. As she spoke, she dumped the contents of the paper bag out on the storage locker and told Brie to help herself. Anna picked up a nut roll and tore open the wrapper. "Dad was in the Navy— that's where he learned to dive. Living out here, he used it mostly for going under and checking out the boat or looking for lost fishing gear. I used to beg him to teach me, and finally, when I was fourteen, he did. After I learned, we used to go out and dive just for fun. Since he died, I haven't done much. There's a rule— you're never supposed to dive alone. But I break it sometimes."

Brie munched a little more of the Snickers bar she'd selected, but her stomach was starting to feel slightly unsettled. So she wrapped up the remainder and, leaning over, tucked it into the pocket of her rain slicker that sat at her feet. Then she flipped the coat over and pulled out a wad of kleenex from the other pocket. The suicide note that she'd placed in her coat up on the bluffs yesterday fell out of the pocket, its message in plain view of Anna.

"Is that the suicide note?" Anna asked, fascinated.

"Yes," said Brie. Feeling uncomfortable, she quickly tucked it back in her pocket. She was agitated with herself. *How could I have forgotten to put it with the other evidence?* The answer, of course, was obvious. The fact was that in the past year since the shooting, she had done a number of things that were out of character for her. She had learned to forgive herself for most of them, but she felt particularly uneasy about having this key piece of evidence with her.

"Well, ready for more hard work?" Anna asked, standing up.

"I'm game," Brie said. "This is a great experience—thanks for inviting me, Anna."

"Hey, you're coming in mighty handy today. Nothing wimpy about you, girl," she said, laughing. "The rest of my traps are down the other side of the island. It'll take about ten minutes to get over there." Anna started to walk back toward the wheel.

"I'm just gonna hang out back here 'til we get there," Brie said. "My stomach's feeling a little off—probably not used to chocolate this early in the morning."

"Could be the motion of the boat, too," Anna said. "You just sit tight—I'll go a little slower."

"Thanks," Brie said. "But I usually don't get seasick, so not to worry."

Back in the wheel house, Anna steered the boat, banking it east-southeast in a long, gradual arc. John's prediction was right. The sea was still rough on this side of the island, with remnants of the gale apparent in the larger-than-normal waves running in from the northeast.

Sitting on the locker, Brie tried to relax, but she had a growing sense of unrest. She was beginning to realize that this wasn't indigestion, but something else. Her gut was trying to get her attention, and she had the distinct feeling that there was something she should be remembering. She wondered whether she should have come today, and if, somehow, she might be needed on the *Maine Wind*.

By 9:30 everyone aboard the *Maine Wind* had finished a breakfast of French toast and bacon and was cleaning up the dishes, when a call came across the radio. DuLac bounded up the companionway and headed aft. As he got closer to the receiver, he recognized Glenn's voice. He grabbed the mike. "This is the *Maine Wind*. Over."

"I've got a call here for Brie from Garrett Parker. Do you want me to patch it through? Over."

"She's not here, Glenn. She went out lobstering this morning with a gal named Anna Stevens. Over."

There was silence at the other end of the radio.

"Over," John repeated.

"Let me sign off with Garrett."

Glenn was back on the radio in seconds. "John, I'm worried about Brie."

"Why, Glenn? What's wrong?"

"That Anna—she's got a mean streak a mile wide. Used to be married to Jack Trudeau, and Pete worked for Jack. It just doesn't feel right, John. Over."

"She never told Brie she was married to Trudeau. What else, Glenn—there's something else, isn't there? Over."

"Trudeau divorced her about a year ago—story was she'd had an affair. I don't put much stock in the island gossip, but the rumor was she tried to kill him one night after the divorce. He never pressed charges, so who knows? I'll tell you one thing, though, I wouldn't want to cross her."

"Over and out." DuLac slammed down the receiver. A picture had been shaping up in his mind. What if Pete, the woman-izer, had an affair with Anna while he lived on the island? Maybe she blamed him for her divorce, or maybe she just decided to give man-killing another try. He didn't know how Tim fit in, but something was terribly wrong. And his concern last night and this morning for Brie's safety? Call it psychic, but it wasn't the sea that was her enemy today.

Rob Lindstrom was just coming up the companionway. John grabbed him by the shirt. "You're coming with me. Get in the yawl boat."

Rob read the urgency in his voice and didn't argue.

"Take charge here, Scott." DuLac climbed over the stern and, within seconds, was in the yawl boat, turning the key. Rob freed the line and they sped across the cove toward a lobsterboat that had just docked.

John spun the boat in a circle near the end of the dock and shouted to a scruffy-looking lobsterman. "Where can I find Jack Trudeau?"

Paulie Tillman gestured out to sea with a hand missing an index finger. "Out there. Haulin' traps."

"Do you know where Anna Stevens has her traps?"

Paulie turned and spewed a mouthful of brown tobacco juice over the side of his boat. "She's got traps up north and over east o' the island."

"You have to take us out there. It's an emergency." John had already thrown a line around one of the dock pilings, and Rob had jumped off the yawl boat.

"Hey, man, what's in it for me?" Paulie smelled a chance for easy money.

Rob stepped across the dock. "A broken nose if you don't get us out there on the double," he said, looming over Paulie.

"Okay, okay. You don't gotta get mean about it." Paulie went forward and turned over the engine of a lobsterboat that looked as unkempt as himself. John and Rob jumped aboard. "Which way?" he asked, pulling away from the wharf.

"East," John said, instinctively. The seas would be high over there. That's where she'd go.

As Brie sat on the locker watching the liquid-silver ocean skimming by, her mind returned to the murder scene and began to focus on the details. The vague feeling of unrest was turning into full-blown apprehension when a disturbing idea entered her head. Another one followed shortly thereafter and another, each causing a click in her consciousness, like tumblers falling into place under the hand of a safecracker. That lobster band next to Pete's body;

he wasn't playing with it, as they had thought, he was trying to leave a clue.

Pete had lived on the island. Anna was pretty—almost beautiful. Pete would have gone after her. The rest Brie could only guess at. Remembering the black traces under Pete's nails, she knelt down on the deck in front of the locker. She glanced briefly over her shoulder before opening the lid. Anna was busy piloting the boat. Quietly, Brie lifted the locker cover and searched for the article she thought might be there. From the corner of the locker she drew out the hood of Anna's wet suit. As she turned it over, her heart jumped into her mouth. Three faint parallel lines were visible on the right side of the black hood, as if the fabric had been slightly compromised. Traces where Pete's fingernails had dug desperately into the hood in his dying moments.

"Planning to go diving?"

Brie whirled around just in time to glimpse something moving toward her head.

She was caught in a riptide, and it was pulling her under. She tried to struggle back to the surface but her hands and feet were bound, and her yellow raincoat became a suit of armor, dragging her farther down. Slowly, slowly she fought her way back to the surface, gasping not for air but for clarity of vision, clarity of mind.

When she finally swam back to consciousness, Brie was surprised to find herself not in the water but still on the deck of the *Just Jake*. Her hands and feet were bound with gray tape, and Anna stood over her, smiling. No longer a smile of friendship, but one of absolute domination. Hatred emanated from her green eyes. Brie sensed that this was no narrow or focused hatred, but one that painted in broad, sweeping strokes large enough to encompass the entire human race. The boat was pitching violently, and she looked around. They were a long way off the island. Brie decided this didn't bode well for her chances of reaching retirement age.

"You know, it's too bad it had to end up this way. I really wasn't planning to kill you when we came out here today. I just wanted to make sure you had the whole thing figured as a murder-suicide. I knew you'd learned about Madie's death from Jack. I made sure I found out everything he told you as soon as you were out of sight of my boat yesterday. He's more scared of me now than when we were married." Her ugly laugh carried over the sounds of the sea.

"You were married to Trudeau? Why didn't he tell me that?"

"For a detective you're not too bright. Jack's brain is in his pants. He figured he'd have a better shot at you if he didn't admit to being divorced. That, and he likes to hide from the fact that we were ever married." The laugh came again. "I'm never going to let him forget, though. Anyway, everything was going fine until your comment about getting the handwriting analyzed. I guess I hadn't figured on that. And then when I saw the note fall out of your pocket, I knew I could get rid of the only piece of evidence connecting me to the crime. So, nothing personal, but our friendship is about to come to an abrupt end."

"But how did you know about Tim?" Brie asked, trying to keep Anna talking while her mind worked on escape.

"Everyone in Lobsterman's Cove knew about him. He used to make his little pilgrimages to the island and go up on the bluffs and mourn for Madie. Then he'd go down to the Two Claws Bar and get drunk. He'd tell his story to anyone who'd listen. I couldn't believe my luck when I saw him carrying Pete's body up to the general store. I thought maybe he'd been planning to kill Pete himself. He'd never have had the guts though. Pathetic loser.

"I knew right then I could make it look like a murder-suicide. So I wrote the note, staked out a spot in the woods near the inn and waited for him to head up to the bluffs. I knew he'd have to go up there, but I hadn't figured on you following him. You almost ruined it for me. When I couldn't scare you off, I hid in the woods up near the cliffs and waited, hoping I'd get a shot at him. Then this other guy showed up, but he didn't stay long. Once I was sure we were alone, it was easy to sneak up on him, what with the noise of the ocean. He was so close to the edge I could have sent him over with one finger."

Brie watched Anna bask in this chance to tell her tale. Like many killers she relished the opportunity to prove her superiority by disclosing all the gruesome facts.

"It's just too bad for all of you that you anchored here to escape the gale. I found out quite accidentally that Pete was on board when I stopped out to sell you the lobsters the first night you arrived. With the dark and the rain he never recognized me. After all, back when I knew him, I was just Jack's wife—didn't have my own lobsterboat. But when I saw *him*, it was like opening an old wound and pouring salt into it. I promised myself three years ago if he ever came back here, I'd kill him.

"So I went back to the wharf, got on my diving gear and swam back out. I snuck aboard while you were all having dinner and disabled the radio to make it harder for you to reach the Coast Guard or any boats in the cove in case things got sticky for me. Then I hid in the hold and waited. Waited, remembering how he'd lied to me, how he told me he loved me, how he promised he'd take me with him when he left the island. I waited there, my hate for him growing with each passing hour—waited for his watch. Waited while he screwed that little dark-haired bitch, knowing he'd used me exactly the same way. While they were having at it, I snuck out of the hold and hid in the shadows. I wasn't alone either—there was another guy up forward watching the whole thing. It was like a freakin' side show. And when she'd finally had enough of him, then it was my turn."

Anna fell silent for a moment as if gathering her energy for the story's climax. Gulls circled overhead crying. Brie saw the madness in her eyes—the same madness she'd seen in the eyes of other killers. She remembered Pete's face during the gale, and knew now that what she'd seen hadn't been fear of the storm, but apprehension that they were sailing to *this* island.

Suddenly Anna was talking again. "He was so far gone after his romp with that little whore that Fred Klemper could have finished him off. I strangled the life out of him, feeling my power return with each ounce of life I squeezed from him. He got a good look at me too. Right at the end I knelt over him and drove that marline spike into his heart, kind of like I was killing a vampire. He wasn't going to suck the life out of any more unsuspecting women. I had a close call too. Right after I'd finished him off, this big hulk of a guy appeared at the back of the ship. I hid a few feet away from Pete, and as soon as he saw the body he took off. I figured he was headed to get the captain, so I climbed over the bow and went down the anchor chain."

So that was the creaking sound Howard had heard over on the starboard side of the ship. All the pieces of the puzzle fit together, but Brie doubted she'd ever get to show it to anyone. Anna, having taken the suicide note from Brie and stuffed it in her own jeans, was filling the large pockets of Brie's raincoat with some kind of lead weights and taping them closed, obviously in preparation for shoving her overboard.

"Time to say goodbye. And if you're smart you'll just go peacefully to the bottom without a fight. It's so much nicer than me running over you with the boat."

Brie pulled her knees into her chest, folding herself into a tight bundle of compressed energy and as Anna started to pull her to her feet, Brie shot up with all the force she could summon, driving her head up under Anna's chin. She heard the crack of Anna's teeth as they slammed together, and she hopped out of the way as Anna crashed backwards onto the deck, unconscious.

It was 9:55 as Paulie Tillman swung his boat north and headed up the eastern side of the island.

"Can't you get any more speed out of this tub?" DuLac shouted into Paulie's ear.

"Insultin' my boat ain't maybe the best way to get where you're goin'. This be as fast as she go. Take it or leave it."

"Sorry." DuLac raised his voice over the ill-tuned engine.

Paulie pointed to a lobsterboat up the shore a ways that was stopped among a flotilla of hot pink buoys. "There's Jack Trudeau. Maybe he's seen her." Paulie continued on his same heading until they were nearly parallel with Trudeau's boat, and then, cutting his motor back, swung slowly in among the glut of colored buoys and maneuvered up to the port side of Trudeau's boat.

"Permission to come aboard," DuLac shouted to Trudeau, who was busy pulling a trap out of the water over on the starboard side of his boat. John didn't wait for a response. Jumping up on the gunwale of Paulie's boat, he sprang across onto the other deck. He was on Jack in a flash, and even though Trudeau was the bigger man, John had surprise and rage working for him. He slammed Jack backward against the wall of the wheelhouse.

"Why did you lie to Brie, you sonofabitch? Why didn't you tell her you were married to Anna Stevens?"

Jack shoved him back. "Get off my boat before I kill you."

"Brie's in danger. She went out with Anna on her boat this morning, and, from what I've just learned about Anna..."

"Why would she go out on a boat with that psycho-bitch? She's dangerous as hell. As soon killya as look atcha."

"We've gotta find her boat, and you'd better pray we're not too late."

"Don't threaten me, you fair-weather sailor."

John bristled but held himself in check.

"I saw her boat headed down this side of the island a while ago," Trudeau said.

"Where'd she go?" John pressed.

"She suddenly veered off and headed east away from the island."

"Where are your binoculars?"

"Up by the wheel."

John darted into the wheelhouse and grabbed them. He began scanning the ocean east of the island. Suddenly he stopped. "There she is, and she's way out there. I only see one person aboard." He nodded urgently toward Paulie's boat. "Is your boat faster than his?"

"Do lobsters crawl into traps?"

"Get over here, Rob," John shouted. "Get us out there as fast as you can, Trudeau."

Trudeau was already at the wheel, and as soon as Rob's feet hit the deck he maneuvered his boat out through the buoys toward open water.

Brie tried to hop toward the wheelhouse, but with her hands and feet taped together she couldn't keep her balance on the pitching deck and fell, landing hard on her right side. She sat up and, turning her back to the wheel, began scooting along the deck. She had to get to the radio and send a Mayday. She could see Anna beginning to stir, and she pushed herself desperately along the deck. Her hands and feet were starting to tingle from lack of circulation, and her head throbbed where Anna had hit her with the gaff. The warm stream of blood she'd felt running down from the wound was starting to dry. She had gotten to the wall of the wheelhouse and pushed herself to her feet. But as she hopped toward the console that held the radio, she heard a sound behind her. Brie spun and took one more jump backwards. Her hands found the console. As Anna took hold of her, Brie grabbed the throttle and gave it a shove, sending the boat surging forward.

Anna flung her across the deck so viciously that Brie felt like a rag doll being slammed to the floor by an angry child. Her head whipped back as she fell and hit the rail. When her vision cleared Anna was standing over her once again, her mouth bleeding profusely, one of her front teeth missing.

But then something else got Brie's attention, and it made her wonder if she were already dead. Her dad was standing a few a feet behind Anna. She saw him there, clear as day, and he seemed to be saying something to her.

"Well, this *has* been fun," Anna jeered, starting to pull Brie to her feet.

Brie wriggled away from her, crabbing her way sideways and trying to focus on her dad—trying to hear what he was saying.

"It's always more exciting when someone puts up a good fight." Her voice had descended to a throaty tremor. "It was actually quite a turn-on the night I killed Pete. He struggled just enough to make it interesting."

Brie could hear her dad now. She could hear him clearly. He was saying, *Remember your strength, Brie. Remember your strength.* She flashed back to her childhood. She was wrestling with her brother, and her dad was standing nearby refereeing, and he was saying, "Remember your strength, Brie. Use your legs."

Anna had her halfway to her feet now and was forcing her over the rail when a large swell lifted the bow of the boat up. Brie fell backwards onto the deck as Anna lurched forward, her upper body thrown across the rail directly above Brie's head. Brie reacted instantly. Pulling her knees into her chest, she shot them up under Anna's hips in one lightning move and thrust with every ounce of strength she could summon. Anna, caught off guard and off balance, went plunging headfirst over the rail into the sea. A moment later Brie felt a sickening thud under the boat and knew that Anna had hit the propeller.

Brie knelt up and looked aft in time to see a reddish pool fading away astern. In the distance she saw a boat rapidly approaching on the same heading.

Just Jake plowed forward, pilotless. Brie pulled herself to her feet and hopped around to face forward. What she saw nearly stopped her heart. The boat was on a collision course with a small island that was not much more than a big pile of rock. As she desperately hopped forward, using the rail for support, she assessed her choices. There were only two, and they were both bleak. Stay aboard and be killed by the impact, or jump overboard and go straight to the bottom with her pockets full of lead.

The increased roar of a motor made her glance over her shoulder. The other boat had almost caught up. Brie saw Trudeau driving and John and Rob poised next to the port rail. The island loomed so close. Brie took two big jumps toward the wheel but, losing her balance, fell to the deck. Trudeau's boat was off the stern now, and a moment more brought it alongside. In the surreal way that things phase into slow motion during a crisis, Brie saw John climb up on the gunwale of Trudeau's boat and jump. A second later Trudeau veered his boat sharply away to starboard. John landed on the deck in a crouch and rolled once before springing to his feet. He ran for the wheelhouse, praying there were no submerged ledges, and swung the wheel so hard to starboard that the boat laid all the way over on her side, veering off the collision course no more than fifteen feet from shore and sending a large bow wave crashing over the rocks.

John pulled the throttle lever to the idle position and went back to Brie. He untaped her hands and feet, picked her up in his arms and carried her to the stern of the boat. She laid her battered head against his shoulder, trying to absorb a little of his strength. He sat down on the stern locker still cradling her in his arms.

"I saw my dad. He was here."

"It's okay, Brie. It's over now. It's okay."

"Thanks, John," she whispered. She left her head on his shoulder, feeling at that moment as if she might just leave it there forever.

"Any time, Brie," he murmured softly.

20

TRUDEAU SWUNG HIS BOAT back alongside the *Just Jake*, and Rob came aboard. He took the wheel and headed them back toward Lobsterman's Cove, leaving John free to tend to Brie. Trudeau went back to search the waters for any sign of Anna's body, but no trace of her was ever found.

John nestled Brie down on the deck next to the locker and went forward to locate the first aid kit he knew Anna would have aboard. He knelt next to Brie, cleaned the blood off her face and checked the head wound.

"She was the most dangerous kind of psychotic," Brie said, wincing as John touched her head. "A really smart one."

"I know," John said. He pressed a thick pad of gauze against the wound. "I think you may need a few stitches, Brie. The Coast Guard should be able to take care of you, or else Scott and I are both trained in first aid."

"I trust you both," Brie murmured. The adrenaline rush had subsided, and she was beginning to feel the first cloying fingers of exhaustion.

As they motored toward the southern end of the island, Rob saw the Coast Guard boat approaching and yelled back to let John know.

"I'm glad they're early. I can't wait to weigh anchor."

"Me either," said Brie. "I'm ready for a change of scene."

"I'll bet."

John sat down next to her in the sun and put an arm around her. Pulling her knees up, Brie curled into him, laying her head on his shoulder and trying not to focus on the pain.

Rob pulled up to an empty dock across from the Coast Guard boat and secured the bow and stern lines.

"I'll go talk to them, Captain," he said.

"Tell them Brie needs first aid."

In minutes three Coast Guardsmen returned with Rob. One of them was carrying a medical kit, and he climbed aboard.

"Hey, how're you doing?" he asked gently, squatting down next to Brie.

"Really happy to be alive," Brie said.

"That's the spirit," he said. He turned to John. "I can take over here, if you want."

"You okay, Brie?" John asked.

"I'm fine. You give them the facts and tell them I'll meet with the police and turn over the film I shot of the crime scene as soon as we get back to the mainland. Just find out where they're bringing the bodies."

"Will do." John stood up and scanned the seas beyond the cove for Trudeau's boat. He wanted to thank Jack, but there was no sign of him. John spotted Paulie Tillman mooring his boat and hailed him. "Thanks for your help, Paulie," he called out. Paulie waved his four-fingered hand in acknowledgement. John and Rob walked off the dock and up toward Fred's store with the other two Coast Guardsmen to collect the bodies.

George served lunch on the deck of the *Maine Wind* before they got underway. There were lots of questions for Brie and lots of speculation about the unknowns of the case.

"Why do you suppose Tim came on the cruise?" Howard asked. "Do you think he meant to harm Pete?"

"I think maybe it was just the opposite," Brie said. "I think he may have come aboard to forgive him. Remember, he was heading for Alaska. I believe he wanted to lay the memory of Madie and the climbing accident to rest at last, and I think forgiving Pete was part of that. And then we ended up here, where she died. That must have been hard for him. When I saw him up on the bluffs yesterday, I think he was saying goodbye to her."

"You know what I can't get over?" George asked Brie when they had a moment alone after lunch.

"What, George?"

"It's the fight Pete and I had the night he died. If he'd let me get the wood out of the hold that night, I would have found Anna hiding there, and Pete would be alive today."

"Maybe. Or maybe she would have added you to her list. Don't forget, George, she was a killer on a mission."

Brie walked over to the rail and looked toward the village. She thought about fate and chance occurrences. Did things happen by design, part of a sometimes-cruel plan, or were they random, like a hand of cards? All she knew was that from the same deck, both death and hope had been dealt. Pete and Tim had been cast, like unsuspecting fish, into Anna's net, and Brie had been pitted in mortal combat against her. This time, though, Brie could see her foe—could change the outcome. And in that fierce struggle she'd saved more than her own life—she'd rescued her *self*. She could now choose to stay or to go back. It was no longer about running away.

At one o'clock DuLac gave the order to raise sail for breaking out the anchor. Brie was still feeling dizzy, so Will carried some life-preserver cushions and a blanket to the stern of the ship, and made a place for her on the deck, out of the wind.

He helped her sit down. "I wanted to let you know I'm no longer interested in the second mate's job—just in case you're wondering," he said.

"I was wondering, but I guess the thought got knocked right out of my head."

"I'm not surprised," Will said. "Anyway, I've decided I'm going to stick around home this summer and help Dad with some repairs on the house."

"That sounds like a good idea, Will. It'll mean a lot to him. You're lucky to still have your dad, you know."

"I know. And I figure he's taken care of me long enough—it's my turn to repay that a little."

Will walked forward and sat down on the cabin top next to his dad. Brie saw him put an arm around Howard's shoulders. Well, I'll be darned, she thought.

As she watched, her shipmates ran up the canvas. When they began to make headway, Scott and Will took turns at the windlass cranking up the anchor. The sails filled, and she heard the now familiar groan of timber as the big schooner leaned into the wind. DuLac spun the ship's wheel and the *Maine Wind* fell off to starboard. They cleared the harbor, and Brie felt her heartbeat quicken as the ocean opened before them, blue with possibility.

DuLac set an easterly course for the mainland. He turned the wheel over to Scott, and walked over and squatted down next to Brie.

"How're you doing?" he asked her.

"It was a pretty good whack on the head. I guess I'm still a little at sea," she joked. "And by the way, since I am, I've decided, for now anyway, maybe sea is the best place for me."

John's face said it all. He laid a hand on her shoulder. "In that case prepare for a fantastic summer."

Brie just smiled. "Aye, Captain."

The *Maine Wind* heeled, her windward deck lifting as she picked up speed, back in her element. Brie felt the sun on her face and in her heart. Two words were written there. *Home Port.*

Author's Note

While *Rigged for Murder* is a work of fiction, and neither Granite Island nor the *Maine Wind* actually exists, I have tried to be as accurate as possible with all details that pertain to the book's Maine coast setting, as well as details and terminology involving sailing and lobstering.

The following sources have been invaluable to me in writing *Rigged*. I would like to acknowledge these authors and their works. *Islands In Time*, by Philip W. Conkling; *The Lobster Chronicles, Life on a Very Small Island*, by Linda Greenlaw; *The Annapolis Book of Seamanship*, by John Rousmaniere; and *Maine Lobsterboats, Builders and Lobstermen Speak of Their Craft*, by Virginia Thorndike.

Finally, I'd like to extend a very special thank you to Captain John Foss of the schooner *American Eagle* and to authors Kit Sloane and G. Miki Hayden for reading *Rigged* and offering their comments for the book jacket.

Visit the author's website at www.windjammermysteries.com.

Coming Soon...

DANGER SECTOR

The Windjammer Mystery Series

JENIFER LECLAIR

Chapter 1

SOUNDS OF OCEAN AND FOREST filled the artist's cottage that occupied a secluded point on the eastern shore of Sentinel Island. Waves slapped the rocky beach below, and just beyond the front door a red squirrel chattered and scolded from its perch in a large spruce tree. Sunlight poured through two roof windows, caressing the honey-hued log walls and burnishing the metal castings and copper sculptures placed around the cabin's great room.

The killer paused a moment and smiled at the tranquility before dragging Amanda's body toward the other end of the room. The socks on her limp feet made a dusty sound against the wide, pine floorboards. In the corner a large aluminum casting of a ship's prow lay overturned, waiting.

The killer began to maneuver her body into the hollow base of the casting. Beads of sweat dampened his chest as he strained under her dead weight. "You should like this, Mandy," he whispered seductively. "You're about to become one with your work. Don't worry, though, I'll be back tonight, and we'll go for a nice ride in your boat."

Retrieving a few slates of scrap wood from Amanda's fireplace kindling box, the killer placed them across the opening, wedging them under the lip of the casting, so the body would stay in place. Unrolling a piece of heavy plastic, he draped it over the base and cut it to the shape of the opening. He began working grey tape around the base. The thick plastic distorted Amanda's wide-eyed stare, giving it a Daliesque twist of horror. Unnerved, the killer's hands began to sweat, making the plastic hard to handle. *It's taking too long. I have to get out of here. Don't panic, you're almost done. Someone could show up. Calm down. There, see, it's finished.*

The killer stood up. Tipping the casting upright with all that weight in the base was easy. He walked over to where Amanda had been sitting, having coffee. He picked the newspaper off the floor, folded it and tossed it onto the table. The killer turned slowly in a circle surveying the room, then left by the back door.

Brie Beaumont shifted on the grey wool blanket. She stretched her arms above her head, laying them on the warm wood of the schooner's deck, so the July sun could get at the underside of them. *What* a *ripe peach of a day—the kind to make you forget that life is chiefly about supply and demand. It demands and you supply.* Eyes closed behind her sunglasses, Brie smiled as the thought drifted lazily through her mind.

She turned her head and studied John DuLac. He'd dozed off lulled by the sun and the motion of the ship at anchor. He was tanned from life at sea, and his dark hair needed a trim. Over the past two months she had come to recognize his presence in her life as a stabilizing force so strong it was almost tangible.

John shifted as she watched him and, rolling onto his left side, opened his eyes. "Hey, you," he said, "I haven't felt this relaxed since I don't know when."

Brie felt a sudden urge to reach out and touch his face, but restrained herself. The beginnings of romance that had blossomed that night in May, on this very deck, had been put on indefinite hold when she had accepted his offer to become second mate aboard the *Maine Wind*. She had been the one to set the boundaries around what would be their working relationship. But the kiss they had shared that night called to her, the memory of it intruding more and more often when he spoke to her, moved past her on deck, sat next to her in the galley at dinner. And now this break in the cruising schedule so they could sail out to Sentinel Island.

Brie hadn't thought much about being along on this junket. After all, she was part of the crew, and she simply assumed the captain needed his three crew members aboard to sail the *Maine Wind* out to the island. But to her surprise, they had dropped anchor mid-day, and John had come up from the galley with a picnic basket and a blanket. When she had asked about Scott and George, she was told they were eating below deck. John had clearly not forgotten that kiss either, and the picnic announced his intention that they'd be sharing these five days as something other than captain and second mate.

Brie knew normally the summer schedule allowed for no such breaks. The cruising season for the Maine windjammers was short, and the captains made the most of the few months they had. But John had left time in this summer's schedule to help his friend, Ben, do some repairs to an old lighthouse he'd inherited out on Sentinel Island.

"Does Ben know when we're arriving?" she asked, staring up at the Atlantic sky.

The motion of the ship, combined with her unearthly view, gave her a distinct and not unpleasureable sense of floating in space and time.

"I didn't give him a definite ETA. He knows better than anyone that we're at the mercy of the prevailing winds. A part of me is eager to get there and see this lighthouse of his..."

"But?"

John propped himself up on his arm and looked at her. "But this is nice too, Detective Beaumont."

Brie pushed her sunglasses up on her head and stared into his unusually brown eyes. "That would be Second Mate Beaumont to you," she said with a smile.

A large cloud passed over the ship, momentarily blocking out the sun and bringing with it a gust of wind that caused Brie to shiver. John leaned across and drew the blanket over her shoulder. He lingered for a moment above her, the electricity between them so strong that Brie felt a crushing sensation in her chest. She'd already decided there was no way she was not kissing him. A wisp of long blond hair had blown across her face, obscuring part of her mouth. He tucked it behind her ear, and at that unfortunate moment the radio crackled to life.

"*Maine Wind, Maine Wind, Maine Wind.*"